A Thriller by

# VICTOR METHOS

1

Richard Miller walked into his home and heard his wife groaning with pleasure. He stood at the front door a long time and listened. She squealed, swore, and grunted. He couldn't remember the last time they'd had sex.

He sat down in the chair next to the door, placing his briefcase on the floor. His palatial estate in one of Honolulu's most expensive neighborhoods was a testament to their marriage. The house had been decorated by a designer Richard didn't like, paid for by a father-in-law he couldn't stand, and kept up by a wife who didn't love him anymore.

On the side table stood a photo of him, his wife, Sharon, and his daughter, Eliza.

Eliza was in middle school and wasn't home yet, but what if she had walked in on her mother? What if she had seen how her mother treated her father? What would that do to a young girl? Richard decided he couldn't let Sharon's transgression stand. Not again.

He marched up the stairs to the master bedroom. The noise grew louder, and he heard multiple voices. The door was open a crack, and he peeked inside.

His wife was in his bed with two men. The men had her bent over, one in front and one behind. Revulsion coursed through him so strongly that he thought he might throw up. And in fact, they only noticed him because he retched. The men didn't even have the courtesy to stop when they saw him.

His wife looked over and rolled her eyes. "Get the hell out, Richard."

"Eliza will be home soon. I don't think you should do these things in our house."

"I said get out!" she screamed, throwing a pillow at him.

He blocked the pillow with the door and stood there. Richard shut the door and slumped against the wall. He pulled his knees to his chest and stared at another family photo, which was hanging on the wall opposite him. He'd thought about divorce more times than he could count, but his house, the cars, Eliza's college fund—Sharon's father paid for all of it. He would get nothing in the divorce, except Eliza. And on his own, what kind of life could he provide for a teenage girl?

Before he could stop them, tears were flowing down his cheeks. He put his hand over his eyes as he heard his wife's screams and the grunts of two strange men, like pigs rolling around his bed.

He could never harm Sharon. Never in a million years. They'd spent fifteen years building a life together. He couldn't purposely hurt her… but he knew there were people who could.

Richard rose, wiped away the tears, and strode out of the house.

Despite being a lawyer, Richard knew nothing about criminal law or the criminal world. He dealt exclusively with tax and estate planning. But one woman in his firm practiced criminal law.

The offices of Strain, Klep & Barnum were on the top floor of the prestigious First Hawaiian Center, the tallest building in the Hawaii Islands. As Richard marched in, the secretary didn't acknowledge him. No one said hello or asked what he was doing back so soon from lunch. His practice stuck him in an office ten hours a day. That didn't leave much time to get to know anyone.

He glanced around as he passed Heather Alana's office. No one inside, and no one around. He went into the office, closed the blinds, and shut the door.

Her computer was password protected, but like most everyone at the office, she always left it open. Richard scanned the folders on his desktop. He found one for closed cases and flipped through them, looking for the right type of case—something involving gratuitous violence.

He found it with an aggravated assault case. A gang member had nearly beaten a man to death in a bar. Heather had gotten the case dismissed because all the witnesses were too scared to show up to court. Richard quickly scanned the man's criminal history. He had a string of robberies, burglaries, assaults, a rape when he was a juvenile, and a homicide charge that had been dismissed because the witness disappeared. It was perfect.

Richard wrote down the man's information on a Post-it then headed out of the office and down to his car, where a meter maid was writing him a parking ticket.

"Oh, no," he said, "no, I was only up for, like, five minutes."

The meter maid rolled her eyes and stuck the ticket under one of the windshield wipers. "Don't do nothin' bad, and nothin' bad'll happen to you."

Richard watched as she lazily strolled back to her car. "That's not true," he said loudly.

He grabbed the ticket, crumpled it up, and threw it on the ground. After a few moments, he picked it up and shoved it into his pocket. He would deal with it later. As he hopped into his car and started the engine, he realized he hadn't felt so energized in… well, since he could remember. His thoughts were clear, and he felt excited and calm all at once. Maybe that was what having a goal did to people.

He drove a good distance inland on the island's main interstate. Why Hawaii had interstates, he couldn't say, but what did he care? People could misname anything. As long as enough people used the term, it would stick.

As he got off the interstate, he realized he didn't spend much time on this part of the island. In fact, he couldn't remember ever being here, even though it was only twenty minutes from his office. The buildings were rundown, and the homes were packed closely together. The Hawaiian natives lived crammed into tight spaces. Everything cost about double what it did on the mainland, but the wages weren't higher. They had to save money where they could.

Richard checked the address again and realized he was on the wrong street. He turned around, slowly rolling through the neighborhoods, until he gave up and put the address into the GPS on his phone. A few minutes later, he stopped in front of the house of Hiapo Makani. He'd never dealt with anyone like Hiapo before.

Could he really do it? The internal debate had been going on since the moment he'd left his house. The image of his wife being used as a sex doll popped into his head. In his bed, in his house, next to photos of him on the nightstand. His stomach churned with bitterness.

Richard got out of the car and looked around. No one was really out. As he walked up to the front porch of the house, he saw an elderly woman on a porch next door. She didn't move. She stared blankly at nothing in particular.

His hand hovered over the door a second. This was it. No going back. He swallowed and knocked.

A heavyset man with tattoos from head to toe answered the door. He was massive, like a wrestler or football player. He scowled at Richard and opened the door wider.

"Are you Hiapo?"

"Who's askin'?"

"My name is Richard Miller… and I'd like to propose a business transaction."

2

Jon Stanton nearly fell off the curb and broke his ankle. He was attempting to sprint at full speed while wearing boots. In two quick hops, he stripped off the boots then continued up the sidewalk.

His legs burned as though his heart were pumping acid. He came to a street and a car blared its horn as he dashed in front of it, barely aware of the fact that he'd almost been hit. As another car turned right in front of him, he jumped over the hood and slid across it on his butt. The driver yelled at him and lay on the horn.

Stanton could see the man up ahead of him, wearing a baseball cap and jeans. The man was younger and faster. If he disappeared into a large crowd, Stanton might not be able to pick him out if he just slipped off the cap. He had to get to him.

yossStanton sprinted down a side street that led to a main road. He held up his badge to the cars that had to slam on their brakes. He raced across the street and turned north. Up ahead and to the left, the man glanced around, probably wondering what had happened to his tail. The man slowed to a trot then began to walk. Stanton kept running.

He got ahead of the man and crossed onto the same side of the street. The man was turned around, scanning the streets behind him. Then he headed inside a convenience store. Probably to hide out in the bathroom until the units chasing him moved on. Not an entirely bad strategy.

Stanton came around to the front of the store just as the other man was walking in. He didn't recognize Stanton, who smiled and held the door open for him. The man was about to walk inside when he glanced down, and saw Stanton's shoeless feet.

Their eyes met. No one moved or spoke… then Stanton reached for his firearm.

The man hit him like a freight train, tackling him to the ground. Several punches hit Stanton before he could move or block them. He moved faster than Stanton could.

Stanton brought up his elbows to protect his face when he felt fingers on his ribs. He was going for Stanton's gun.

The man wrapped his hand around Stanton's Desert Eagle and tugged. But Stanton's special detective's holster kept it in place. Stanton wrapped his arms around the man's biceps, pinning his arms to his body. Lifting with his hips, he spun so the man was on his back, with Stanton on top of him.

Stanton cocked his arm back. With all his bodyweight behind it, he dropped an elbow into the man's cheek. The vicious blow bounced the man's head off the pavement.

Stanton knocked him again, in the same spot. The man groaned as police cars screeched to a stop in the convenience store parking lot. It was complete confusion at first. The uniformed officers didn't recognize Stanton, and they had their weapons drawn on him.

"I'm with HPD. I'm in the homicide detail. Jon Stanton."

"Shut the hell up!"

Finally, a uniform who'd met him before arrived and recognized him. Stanton was allowed to move, and three uniforms converged on the man then spun him around, slapping cuffs on his wrists. Stanton rose and wiped the blood from his nose. He was thirty-seven years old. What was he doing in this situation?

Connor Jones, a junior detective with the homicide detail, showed up in his new Dodge Charger. He strolled over with a smile as he saw the man lifted and shoved into the back of a police cruiser.

"You chased him down without shoes?" Jones asked.

"Best way to run." Stanton leaned down, placing his palms on his knees. Age had a way of sucking the body's ability to recover, and Stanton was feeling the full effects of the chase.

"You all right?"

Stanton shook his head and spit. He thought he might throw up. "Do me a favor, would you Connor? Go inside and buy me some water and Tums."

Stanton stopped his Jeep outside the precinct, which was in district one, Central Honolulu on the island of Oahu. It had more murders, rapes, burglaries, and assaults than all the other districts in the state. Kai, Stanton's captain, had purposely selected him for the district when he'd hired him. Being a lateral hire meant Stanton got credit for his decade with the San Diego Police Department, along with a massive pay bump and a boost to his pension.

Stanton sauntered across the street and into the building. Opposite the precinct was an actual palace, the last left in the United States. It had been used by the royalty of Hawaii, and he could picture armies surrounding it, a royal court, concubines, and court intrigue. But it had become little more than a tourist destination visited by only a few people a day.

Stanton nodded to the sole uniform at the reception desk then took the elevator to the fifth floor. As he rode, he rubbed his swollen jaw, which matched his puffy eye and lip. He tried not to show how much it bothered him—both that he been beaten up and that just a few hits could hurt him so badly—as he stepped off the elevator and made his way to Interrogation Five, the last and quietest interrogation room.

Inside, David Bristol sat handcuffed to a chair. The room was gray, as were the desk and chairs. Stanton shut the door and sat across from him. In the corner, a camera's red recording light blinked.

"How's the jaw?" David asked.

"Sore. How's the cheek?"

"I think you broke it, man. Hurts like a sonofabitch. I'm thinkin' lawsuit, man."

"Feel free," Stanton said. "I don't have any money to take." He placed his hands on the table. "You didn't have to run, David."

"Yeah, I did. My cousin, up there in Fresno, man, he got shot down by the cops for havin' an eight ball of H, man. And that's the truth. Shit goes down when you get harassed by the cops."

"I wasn't harassing you."

"Hell yes, you was. What you call showin' up at a man's house and kickin' down his door?"

"We had a warrant. We know you killed him."

"Shee-at, I ain't killed nobody."

Stanton grinned. "I walked through your landlord's apartment next to yours and noticed something odd. His bed was missing a mattress. The box spring was there, but not the mattress. So I called down to the dump and asked if anyone had dumped a mattress the past couple of days. What do you think they told me, David?"

David's eyes dropped to the table. He was silent for a long time.

"I found him, David. It wasn't fun. I had to dig through piles of refuse to do it. But I found him. That was clever of you to cut open your mattress and shove him inside. No one would have even noticed. It would have just been buried among the mountains of garbage. And I found something else that was odd. A knife. A large kitchen knife, which I had run for prints. Whose prints do you think came back?"

He shrugged but didn't say anything.

"You gotta wear gloves. How could you do something like this and not wear gloves? Don't you watch *CSI?*"

"Man, fuck that asshole, man."

"What'd he do to you?"

"I was late on the damn rent, man. So that fucker went to my place and took all my shit—and I mean *all* my shit—and put it in storage. And he said I couldn't get it back until I paid the rent, man. Fuck him."

"That must've been fun to stab him over and over like that. In his own house, too."

He smiled. "Yeah, man. He was just screamin' like a bitch, man. Weren't so tough then."

Stanton grinned and rose. "I appreciate you talking to me, David."

As Stanton exited the room, he saw Kai standing at the one-way glass. The big man had his arms folded and a smile on his face.

"Nice work," Kai said.

"He wanted to talk. I don't think he realizes how serious murder is."

Kai shook his head. "Weird juju, my friend. When people don't think killing another person is a big deal."

Stanton stepped over to the one-way glass and looked in. David had rested his forehead on the table. "We got everything we need. Who Mirandized him?"

"Jones, right before you walked in."

"Have Jones finish up with the details."

Stanton began walking out when Kai shouted, "Where you goin'?"

"To the hospital. I think he fractured my jaw."

3

The home was decorated in native Hawaiian décor, a lot of religious and ocean stuff, and it smelled like cooking pork, though nothing was on the stove. Richard Miller sat awkwardly at the table. Across from him, Hiapo Makani sat eyeing him.

Hiapo couldn't really follow along with a decent conversation. He needed help, so he'd called his friend Tate Reynolds to come over. He and Hiapo were simply waiting.

But they'd been waiting for twenty minutes without speaking a word to each other. Richard finally cleared his throat and said, "So, you like sports?"

Hiapo didn't move or change his expression. His eyes were fixed on Richard as though he were a piece of meat and dinnertime just had to come around before he could dig in. Richard cleared his throat again and looked around the house once more.

Another twenty-five minutes later, there was a knock at the door. Tate Reynolds was shorter and thinner than Hiapo, but he looked more mischievous, maybe because of the black butterfly tattoos on his wrists. He was white, but every space available on his skin had been taken up with dark tattoos, as though he were trying to cover up his skin color.

Tate sat at the table and lit a cigarette. He took a few puffs before he said, "So what do you want, little man?" Tate's enunciation was clear. No hint of an accent or street slang. He sounded educated.

"Hiapo didn't tell you?"

"He did. But I want to hear it from you."

Richard swallowed, unable to look the men in the eyes. "I want you to kill my wife."

Tate glanced at Hiapo, who looked at him only by moving his eyes. Neither man said anything as the smoke whirled between them. Richard coughed and waved away the acrid smoke. It smelled closer to burnt rubber than tobacco.

"Why do you want to kill her?" Tate asked.

"That's personal. You guys just need to know that it needs to get done."

"Personal, huh? Why not just divorce her?"

"Again, that's personal. So do you think you can do it?"

Tate took a puff of his cigarette. "No, I think I've spent enough time in Halawa. Hiapo here just got out. We're not looking to go back. Now I think you need to leave, little man."

"Well, please, I mean… listen if you can do this—"

Tate shot to his feet, grabbed Richard by the collar, and began dragging him out of the house.

"No," Richard said, "please. Listen, listen! I'll pay you a hundred thousand dollars."

Tate stopped, seemingly frozen in place. He looked back at Hiapo then at Richard. "Where are you gonna get a hundred K?"

"I can get it. Our family's wealthy. Well, her family. I can get it."

"Fine, payment up front."

Richard laughed. Tate let go of his collar, and Richard straightened himself. "I wasn't born yesterday. We'll have to figure something else out."

"Like what?"

"I'll put the money in an escrow account under your name with a provision that says the funds will be released to you on a certain date. If the deed is done by then, the funds get released. If it's not, I can cancel the release. But the money will be in your name."

Tate blew out a puff of smoke into Richard's face, causing him to cough again.

"A hundred K, just for her?"

"Yup."

He looked to Hiapo, who didn't move or speak.

"All right, little man. You got yourself a deal."


Driving home, Richard thought he should have felt some sort of elation, maybe relief that things were in motion. But nothing came to him—nothing but a gray heaviness in his gut, as if he'd just eaten a large meal that didn't agree with him.

He thought back to their wedding. Sharon looked so beautiful in her backless dress that he'd kept asking himself how a guy like him could land a girl like her. The first few years had been great. Lots of conversations and trips. Their first and only child. Eliza had been born on a Friday. He remembered that because he'd missed his favorite show at the time, *Battlestar Galactica*, to be at the hospital.

When he arrived home, he ambled through the door. "Hello?"

No one responded. Eliza should have been home, but she'd probably left with her friends. Richard didn't blame her. He would probably want to be somewhere else if he were a teenage girl.

After taking the stairs two at a time, he found Sharon sitting at the mirror in their bedroom. She was applying makeup, and her hair was still wet from a shower. He stood by the door, watching her. His heart hurt. When he saw her, he saw the woman in the wedding dress. But when she saw him, she saw something else. And he didn't know what.

"Do you want me to pick something up for dinner?" he asked.

"No, I'm going out."

"Where?"

"With the girls. I won't be back tonight."

He hesitated. "To another swingers' party?"

"*Swinger* is such an antiquated word, Richard. Can you not be such a dork for even a second?"

He looked down at the floor. For a long time, neither of them spoke. "There was a time when you loved me. I remember it. I remember your face would light up when I walked into a room. What happened to that girl, Shar?"

She stopped applying her makeup for a moment. A temporary hesitation. "She grew up."

"Do you not care how much it hurts me?"

"So get a divorce. Oh, wait. You won't do that, will you? Because you'll lose all of this. All the money and the cars and the houses. That's all you married me for anyway."

"That's not true, and you know it, damn it. I loved you."

"Get over yourself, Richard."

"Can you just… I mean, our daughter lives here. Can you not bring those men here like that?"

"It's my house. I'll do whatever I damn well please."

She rose, and her robe flapped open. She was wearing nothing underneath. She saw him look at her breasts, and she closed it again.

"Really?" he said. "You flash your tits to any stranger that gives you a smile, but you close your robe to your husband? Why don't you just divorce me?"

"Because for some fucking reason Daddy thinks we need to be a family for his granddaughter. That's all he ever talks about. His granddaughter. And what Daddy says goes. At least until the old fucker dies."

The massive walk-in closet was full of clothing from top to bottom. Richard watched Sharon get dressed. She wore tight leather pants and knee-high boots. Her top accentuated her breasts and exposed her muscular arms.

Richard sighed. "Do you love us at all anymore? Does your husband or daughter mean anything to you, Sharon?"

"Make sure she doesn't miss school tomorrow. She's going to get kicked out if she gets any more absences." She brushed past him. And with that, she was gone.

Richard's heavy gray feeling was replaced by something else: certainty. And it felt good. For once, in as long as he could remember, he felt certain about something.

4

Stanton finished his paperwork early so that he could make his appointment. As he was heading out of the bullpen, Kai ambled out and stopped him.

"Want you to meet someone," he said.

Stanton had met Kai when they both started as uniforms with the San Diego Police Department. A former Chargers linebacker who'd blown out his knee, Kai had been huge even back then. Stanton had felt an instant kinship with him, and Kai was the one who had convinced him to move to Hawaii.

Stanton tried to show him the formality and respect due his captain, but that was difficult since he and Stanton had come up and learned the streets together. He saw Kai as an equal, and Stanton wondered if he would be in a higher position right now if he'd played the political game better.

A skinny woman was sitting in front of Kai's desk. She was native, brown with black, silky hair that came down to her shoulders. Her sleeveless shirt revealed arms covered with tattoos from wrists to shoulders, depicting intricate dragons and native warriors in fierce poses.

She smiled at Stanton, rose, and shook his hand.

"This is Laka Alemea. She's gonna be your new partner."

Stanton looked at Kai then back at Laka. "Nice to meet you," he said.

"You, too. I've heard a lot about you."

Stanton grinned. "All good, I hope. Can I talk to you for a sec, Kai?"

Kai followed him out of the office, leaving Laka staring at the certificates on his walls.

"You know I don't work with a partner," Stanton said.

"I know. Lone wolf and all. But you need a partner, man. You all alone out there. And I think she'll be good for you." Kai glanced at her then turned back to Stanton. "And she's cute, ain't she? She's also my niece."

"That's your niece?"

"What? She too good-lookin' to be related to me?"

"Well… yeah."

Kai shook his head. "That's what I get for doin' somethin' nice for you. She's your partner. I see you here late every night. No one to go home to. You need this, bra. And she needs a good man and to stop dating those assholes she's been dating."

Stanton watched the young woman. She wore almost no makeup. She was quite attractive. "Fine, a partner. Just probationary."

"Sure, whatever."

Stanton turned and headed out of the building. He looked back at Kai, who was grinning as he walked back to his office. Though Stanton couldn't quite figure out why, Kai had always had a soft spot in his heart for him. He'd come up with twenty other officers and didn't have any contact with them. He'd never asked any of them to move to Hawaii or offered them a job under him.

The sun was hot as Stanton left the precinct and strolled to his Jeep. When he got in, he blared George Michael on his iPhone connected to the stereo and pulled onto the streets of Honolulu. The island felt completely different from San Diego. But it had an underbelly, like anywhere else. At night, the prostitutes came out to the tourist locations and downtown. Prostitution had existed in such a degree for so long because of the proximity of the naval bases that the police largely ignored it. When he drove the streets at night, he saw the girls, some as young as ten, selling themselves to men who came to the islands just for the prostitutes.

Drugs, of course, were sold on about every corner and hotel bar, day or night. And again, the police largely ignored it when tourists were involved.

Serial murder, though not as prominent in Oahu as in California, occurred more frequently than it should have, given Oahu's smaller population. The island was sunshine and smiles during the day, but at night, it became a playground for indulging in darker desires.

He drove to the medical center and parked in patient parking with a few minutes to spare. He finished the song he was listening to then went inside the building.

Stanton sat in the third-floor waiting room for Dr. Natalia Vaquer, the third psychiatrist he had been to in his life. She had helped him through his failed engagement with Emma and both his sons moving away from him to live with their mother in Boston. Stanton had gone from having his family with him in paradise to being completely alone.

The double doors leading back to her office opened, and Dr. Vaquer smiled at him.

"Jon, good to see you. Come back, please."

Stanton followed her in and sat on the couch in the center of the room as she took a seat in a recliner. She pulled down her skirt and got out an iPad and a stylus to take notes.

"They're giving me a partner," Stanton said, skipping the chit-chat.

"Really? It was my understanding that you preferred to work alone."

"I did. I do. But my captain thinks it'll be good for me to have a partner. He thinks I spend too much time alone."

"We've spoken often about your inclination toward solitude. Now that your sons have moved, do you still feel that inclination?"

"I don't know. Mathew, my oldest, is supposed to move out here. But he said that last year, too. I think he has a girlfriend he doesn't want to leave. But sometimes, I really wish he would come out. Other times, I don't."

"Why not?"

"The line of work I'm in. That's why they moved in the first place. That's what ruined my marriage and then my engagement. Always the work."

"I've heard you use a term before that I wanted to speak about, Jon. Blood work. I heard you say that."

"Just a term homicide detectives use to describe murder."

"Does it ever affect you? Seeing all that blood and gore?"

Stanton leaned back into the couch, a bit more at ease. "I didn't think it did, but sometimes, I see parents let their teenagers go to the mall by themselves, and I wonder how they can possibly do it. It's a perfectly normal thing, but the only thing I can think about when I see that is their body in a ditch or tied up in some basement."

"That can't be very calming, to see only images of violence like that."

"I don't know." He paused. "I can't really remember a time I didn't think this way."

"Because of your sister?"

Just the word *sister* brought up memories Stanton wanted buried. He'd seen victims bury everything from rape to the death of a loved one. But he couldn't do it. His fifteen-year-old sister had disappeared from a movie theater in Seattle, where he grew up. No leads, no body—nothing. It had nearly destroyed his parents. For a long time, he'd thought his sister's disappearance hadn't affected him. But looking back on his life, his inability to form close relationships, his line of work… everything seemed to point to that single event.

"Probably," he said. "My father was distant, and my mother was passive. I didn't interact much with them. My sister was who basically raised me. When she disappeared, I had no one. I'd see her places for years afterward. At a grocery store or the airport… I thought I was going crazy. It wasn't until I turned eighteen that it stopped."

"What happened at eighteen?"

"I don't know. I guess you'd call it a walkabout or something. I was reading a lot of Conrad and Hemingway at the time. That idea of finding yourself and becoming a man. I left my parents and lived in a shack on the beach with twenty other lost kids. I bummed around Mexico for a while, parts of Central America. I thought about going to war, but it was one of the rare times in American history where we happened not to be at war."

She grinned. "I don't see you in combat."

"No, I don't think taking orders would have sat well with me. Neither would killing someone just because I was told to do it. In Vietnam, only about thirty percent of the soldiers actually fired their weapons with the intent to kill the enemy. Most were missing on purpose or closing their eyes. They didn't want to be there and didn't believe in the cause."

"Jon, I have never really mentioned anything about your doctorate in psychology, but one thing I have seen is a keen insight into everything and everyone, except yourself. You look at a murder scene and see things other people don't. Events in history, which we've spoken about before, are the same way. I learn something just listening to you speak about them. But when it comes to you, Jon Stanton, and your own life, that perception seems to shut down. Why is that?"

Stanton rubbed the edge of his finger. A bit of eczema, which he'd never had in his life, had appeared there. The dermatologist told him that either an irritant or stress had caused the inflammation.

"Do you see a psychiatrist, Dr. Vaquer?"

"This isn't about me."

"I know, but my point is that I bet you do. Almost all mental health professionals do. Have you ever asked why that is?"

She nodded. "We all lack perception into ourselves."

"And that's why we go into the mental health professions. To see if we can find that perception."

She shifted in her seat and wrote something on her iPad. "Have you thought any more about our conversation about leaving police work?"

He shook his head. "I can't do anything else. I was a mediocre professor, and I'd be an even worse therapist. Police work is the only thing I'm good at."

"Police work or blood work?"

He didn't say anything. Instead, he laid his head back on the couch and stared at the ceiling.

When the session was over, Stanton was exhausted. He always was, even though he did nothing more than sit on a couch and answer questions. Stanton believed in different forms of energy, and mental energy was certainly one of the most powerful. The mental energy he expended every time he sat in Dr. Vaquer's office was enormous. But it came with a reward. After most sessions, he hit the ocean.

Oahu had some of the best surfing in the world, one of the main selling points for Stanton. Not half an hour from his house was the North Shore, one of the best surfing spots on the island.

Stanton suited up. Rather than running home to grab his board, he decided to rent one, maybe something other his standard shortboard. The waves were so-so, and he thought a hybrid board would be better suited to catch a decent wave.

The wetsuit, still damp from the day before, chilled his skin. He zipped it up and lay on the sand, keeping his eyes closed and absorbing the sunlight's dull-red glow. The sun rejuvenated him, strengthened him. Whenever he felt like collapsing from exhaustion, whether mental or physical, the sunlight and the ocean kept him going. Wherever he was or whatever he was doing, he made time for the ocean.

As he paddled out, he felt the coolness of the sea. The water tasted salty as it splashed up into his face. He let his fingers dangle a long time before each stroke, absorbing the calmness of the moment.

When he was far enough out, he turned back to the shore and lightly rode the waves before unleashing a fury of paddling. Right at the cusp of letting the momentum tip him over, he flipped up with both feet then felt the stretch in his legs as he crouched. He cut to the left then spun the board into a vertical position. The wave was forgiving, guiding him through his movements. That was the key to surfing that took some people decades to learn: the surfer isn't in charge. The ocean is. The surfer has to give in and work in harmony or be swallowed up like a speck of dust.

Stanton surfed a solid hour before taking a break to get a drink. Tucked underneath his towel on the beach, his cell phone vibrated as he sat in the sand and sipped from a water bottle.

He had a single text message from dispatch letting him know he'd caught a new homicide. As he rose to shower and dress, he remembered his new partner. Somehow, the burden of catching a new case seemed lighter. Someone else would be there, taking in the horror of the scene and splitting the work. He thought that maybe Kai understood him better than he understood himself.

5

The bar was about the shadiest place Richard Miller had ever been to. He stepped through the doorway and was immediately overwhelmed by the stench of marijuana, cigarettes, vomit, spilt alcohol, and Lord knew what else. He thought right then and there about turning around and heading home. His marriage wasn't really so bad after all, was it? He could live with the infidelity… but the cruelty was something else. She wasn't subtle about anything. He still loved her, but she loathed him.

Tate Reynolds, Hiapo, and a new fella he hadn't met before were sitting at a booth away from the other customers. Richard smiled and waved to them. None of them waved back.

He strolled over, stopping a waitress to ask for a beer. He never drank beer, but he wanted to seem like one of the boys. Just an average Joe out for his nightcap.

"Hi, guys," he said.

Tate sucked on a cigarette, his eyes narrow and rimmed with red as he stared up at Richard. The group was silent, so Richard helped himself to a seat. Tate passed the cigarette over to Hiapo, who took some puffs then gave it to the third man.

"So," Tate said, blowing out a puff of smoke into Richard's face, "what do you got?"

"Yoga," Richard said.

"Yoga?"

"Yes, yoga. Three evenings a week, she goes to a yoga class. It's in this, like, strip mall, I guess you'd call it. But not really a strip mall. It's a little trendy place. There's a Middle Eastern restaurant next to it. Lebanese. Their kabob is to die for. You really should try it if you're ever out there. Um, where was I? Oh, and across the street is a gay shop."

"What the fuck is a gay shop?"

"They have, like, gay sex toys and things. Right next to that is a coffee shop. Anyway, the reason I'm telling you all that is because the parking is terrible. All those stores are too close to each other. So you have to go to this back parking lot to access any of them. By the time she gets out of her yoga class, it's dark. And there aren't many people back there."

"She got mace or a gun or anything?"

"No, she's not like that. She grew up rich and doesn't know what people are capable of. Nothing really bad's ever happened to her. She won't see you coming at all."

The cigarette came back to Tate, and he let it dangle between his lips. The burnt-rubber smell was still there, and Richard wondered what was in the cigarette.

Tate leaned back in the seat, squinting against the smoke from the cigarette. "And we just do it there, huh?"

"No," Richard said, pulling out a set of keys. He placed them in the center of the table. "An RV. Take her in that. There's an RV park across the island near the North Shore. Brand-new, bought under a fake name. You can leave her and the RV there. No one will even notice for a few weeks. Maybe months."

Tate looked to Hiapo, who shrugged. "What about the money?"

Richard took out a slip of paper and slid it to him. "This is the escrow account number at the bank. You can go to the bank anytime and ask them how much is in there and what the details are. Basically, it will be released to you two weeks from today. The only way it won't be released is if I don't call in the day before for final authorization. And the only way I wouldn't do that is if the job isn't done."

"How do I know you won't just cancel it anyway?"

"Gentlemen," he said, glancing at each of them, "all of you know what I look like and my name. You could look me up in the phone book and get my address. I'm not risking crossing you over money that doesn't mean anything to me. I'll have more money than I know what to do with once she's gone. So I'm not looking to cross anybody here. I just want it done and over with and to move on with my life."

The three men looked at each other before Tate said, "Okay. When's she at yoga next?"

Sharon Miller sat in the back of the club, where the lighting was a dim red. Cut off from the rest of the club and certainly the bar, the room was used almost exclusively for sex, though sometimes, it was used for ingesting enormous amounts of drugs—coke, mostly. She lay on a couch, watching as two of her friends had sex with a native guy covered in tattoos. Both her friends were married, and their husbands were at the club somewhere, though she didn't see them at the moment.

Sharon hadn't been laid the entire night. She didn't feel into it. Something about the way she and Richard had left off nagged at her. He was right. At one time, they had been inseparable. They were so in love, it hurt. She remembered how he'd smiled whenever she entered a room. One of the saddest things about the situation was that he still smiled when he saw her, though there was nothing between them any longer.

She took a shot of tequila from a glass on the side table next to her then rose. She would have told her friends she was leaving, but they had their hands full.

The night air was warm, and she glanced at the moon. It was nearly full, just a little tip of it covered with the blackness of night. Her phone buzzed as she walked to her car. Her daughter, Eliza, had texted, asking when she would be home. She didn't reply. Instead, she got into the car, and decided to drive to her boyfriend's house.

The home was situated on a full acre near the beach. White with deep-blue trim, it reminded her of the princess castles she'd seen on cartoons as a child. A perfect fairy tale. But if that were true, she guessed she wouldn't have felt that gnawing sensation in her gut every time she pulled up to his house.

She parked in the driveway and slowly paced around the lawn, taking in the starlit sky. She didn't want to be inside just yet.

"I thought that was you."

Her boyfriend, Jorge, was seated on a second-floor balcony overlooking the lawn. He smiled at her as he took a sip of wine.

"I didn't want to go home just yet," she said.

"This is your home. Whenever you want it to be."

"I'm not ready for that yet."

"Up to you. I just want you to know I'm here whenever you want me."

She sat down on the lawn and leaned back on her hands. Jorge was handsome, young, and strong in a way Richard never had been. Jorge took what he wanted out of life and fought like hell when he didn't get it. Richard was passive and seemed happy with whatever scraps were given to him. The fact that her husband and lover were polar opposites wasn't lost on her.

"Do you get jealous?" she asked.

"Of what?"

"Knowing I'm with other men."

"Like your husband?"

"I haven't been with my husband in nearly two years. But you know I love sex."

He nodded. "I know. And no, I don't get jealous."

"Why not?"

"Because I have other women, as well. That would be quite hypocritical of me, wouldn't it?"

She looked up to the stars. "Do you think it's wrong? The way I treat him?"

"I think he puts up with what he's willing to put up with."

"That doesn't make any sense."

He sipped his wine and shrugged. "What the hell do I know? I'm drunk."

"I think… it might be time to leave him soon."

"How soon?"

"I don't know. But this arrangement isn't good for either one of us. I think it'd be better if we severed the ties cleanly. Hopefully, my father will get over it. He told me if I divorced and left them, I wouldn't see a dime. But maybe when he sees it isn't working and it's better for Eliza that we be separated, he'll change his mind."

He lifted his glass. "I'll drink to that." Jorge finished the wine and rose. "Now get into my bed."

She smiled and stood up, her eyes never leaving his as she strolled into the house.

6

Stanton rolled to a stop at a scene he'd been to hundreds of times. The yellow police tape reflected the red and blues. The Crime Scene Unit—or as it was called in the Honolulu PD, the Scientific Investigation Section—had already set up and was surveying the scene. The camera flashes seemed just a little out of date. He'd been there before, in his dreams and in his waking hours.

He stepped out of the car and saw Laka's slender figure leaning against a white Ford Taurus. She was wearing suit pants and had her hands in her pockets. Her badge swung lightly on a lanyard around her neck.

"I was waiting for you," she said, walking up to him.

"What do we have?"

"Caucasian male, thrown from a second-story window. We found glass all around him."

A nude male lay flat in the street, blood pooled around him. He had a severe injury to the top of his skull, probably blunt-force trauma. Stanton looked up at the hotel building behind the body. A window had been broken out on the second floor.

"Was the majority of the glass found outside?"

"Yeah. Definitely thrown from the inside out."

"Who's the vic?"

"Steven Jay Fritts. He's a local. Works at the Four Seasons as a server."

Stanton approached the body. Since he had no gloves or booties, he didn't want to touch anything. Unlike the portrayal on television, contaminating crime scenes was a serious problem in every homicide. The wind, passersby, the weather, and an entire host of external factors had already contaminated the scene by the time the police arrived. Stanton was always careful not to add to that.

"Who called it in?" Stanton asked.

"Steven's boyfriend. He's over there."

The skinny man was wearing a jacket, though it wasn't cold. Looking pale, he appeared shaken up, and his eyes were darting back and forth. Stanton approached him and noticed Laka stayed beside him.

"I'm Detective Jon Stanton with the Honolulu PD. My understanding is you're Steven's boyfriend," Stanton said.

"Yeah... yeah, I am. I mean... I was."

"I'm sorry about what happened."

"Yeah... well, yeah."

"So what did you see?"

The man swallowed, unable to take his eyes off the body in the road. Stanton stepped between him and the body, blocking his view.

"I got in around five, and… I don't know. He was upset about something. So I left him. We got into a fight about it. I asked him why he was acting that way, and he wouldn't tell me. So I just took a shower, and I hear this, like, crash. I came out, and he was on the street."

"Did you see anyone running away from the scene?"

He shook his head. "No."

"Was anyone else in the hotel room with you two?"

"No, it was just us. And I checked the door after, and it was locked. I don't… I don't know what could've happened."

Stanton nodded and looked at the hotel. "I'll be right back."

Laka followed him into the hotel. Stanton hadn't had a partner for so long that having one felt uncomfortable, as though he'd been assigned a babysitter. But he didn't say anything. Laka seemed friendly, and he didn't wish to be aloof with her.

"How long have you been with Homicide?" Stanton asked.

"Um, about a week."

Stanton stopped and turned to her. "This is your first case?"

"Yeah. I thought Kai told you."

"No, he didn't mention that."

"Is it a problem?"

"No, not really. Let's head up to the room."

Stanton had assumed altruistic motives behind Kai's forcing him to accept Laka as a partner, but perhaps that wasn't the case. She would have to be trained, and Kai apparently wanted Stanton to train her. At the San Diego PD, his captains and lieutenants wanted new detectives as far away from him as they could get.

They took the elevator to the second floor, where a uniform was standing outside the hotel room. Stanton had met the young man before. They nodded to each other as he stepped inside the room.

One large couch, a flat-screen television on the wall, a fridge, and almost nothing else filled the room. The room was sparse to the point of appearing unfinished. Stanton paced the room slowly. Nothing seemed out of place. His eyes moved to the bedroom, and he walked inside. The window was there, broken out. It was large, at least four foot by five foot. He peered through the hole and down at the pavement.

"He could've fallen," Laka offered.

"When you fall, you fall straight down. If you're thrown or jump, you fall in an arch. He's far enough away from the building that he fell in an arch. So he was either thrown or jumped out of the window. Guessing from the massive wound on his head, I don't think he jumped."

"The boyfriend?"

"That would be my guess. Can you have one of the uniforms search the trash in the hotel? The dumpster outside, too. I want them to look for a blunt object that has any blood or hair on it. Maybe a statuette, something you'd find in a hotel room."

"On it."

Stanton sat down on the edge of the bed. He stared out at the moon through the broken glass. His eyes led him down and around the room, then back to the bathroom. He went in and flipped on the light. The linoleum floors glistened from a recent cleaning. Stanton looked at himself in the mirror. More and more, he saw his father. And it frightened him.

If the boyfriend was responsible, there was something there that would tell Stanton. No one could remember every detail. When covering up a crime, people panicked. Panic released a hormone called cortisol into the blood. It affected memory, adrenaline release, and blood sugar. With all of those things misfiring at once, thinking became more difficult. That's why standardized tests in school were such a poor indicator of success or intelligence: The day of a test was the worst day to attempt to measure anyone's abilities.

Stanton opened the frosted glass door of the shower. Water glistened in the tub and on the tiled wall. He ran his eyes up to the showerhead and placed his finger on it. It was still damp. The boyfriend had either really been taking a shower or ran the shower after the argument and bludgeoning the victim, but probably before throwing him out the window. He needed time to try to clean up first.

*I strike him. I'm so angry. Just balled-up fury. I can't believe he's doing this to me. I grab the nearest thing available and bash his head with it. It surprises me how easy it is. The head caves like a melon, and I'm standing over this bleeding body. What have I done now? Everyone knows we're here together. People have seen us. People know we're here.*

*The hotel has a camera in the lobby, so I can't say I was out. But I can say I was in the hall or in the shower. The shower would be just enough that no one could contradict me. I turn on the shower in case anyone checks it. Then I take his body. I lift it in my arms. He's so heavy. He's never been this heavy before. I throw his body out the window, shattering it. Bits of glass fly over me. The body falls, and I quickly turn the shower off. I come out to the window, act shocked, and call the police… but I don't…*

Stanton hadn't even realized his eyes were closed. He opened them slowly, readjusting to the level of light in the bathroom. Then he ran his fingers over both towels hanging next to the shower. Bone dry. No one had used them to towel off.

Stanton left the room and headed back downstairs. He didn't want the boyfriend to run, so he motioned for two uniforms to join him. Signaling for them to go around to the front of the man, he went up behind the boyfriend. "Excuse me."

"Yes?" the man said.

"Just some follow-up questions if it's okay."

"Yeah… I mean, yeah. Yes, that's fine."

"What was your name again?"

"Russell. Um, Neal. Russell Neal."

"And you're just visiting the island, I'm guessing."

"Yeah, yeah, we're from Los Angeles."

Stanton nodded. He maintained eye contact during the silence, seeing how Russell would react. The young man began to fidget.

"Well, I'm afraid the body was thrown from the window. He didn't fall. And it looks like he took a nasty blow to the head before being thrown down. The blow is likely what killed him. We found something, though."

"What?"

"Nothing you need to concern yourself with. But we think it was used to bash in his skull. It's being tested for prints and DNA right now."

"Where did you…"

"Find it? Yeah, we have our ways. So just hang tight. We're running the prints through IAFIS right now and should get a hit soon. But if they cleaned it up, the DNA will still be there. The only thing that removes that is bleach, and we didn't see any in the room."

The man swallowed. "But, I mean, if whoever did this isn't in the system, you won't find him. Will you?"

"Oh, yeah. Everyone gets their fingerprints taken at birth, and those prints go into IAFIS. It's the FBI's database. So as long as they were born in the United States, we'll have a hit in about ten minutes. Sit tight. We'll know soon."

Stanton turned and saw Laka standing there with a grin. They sauntered up to the hotel entrance and took a seat on a wooden bench.

"Nice touch," she said. "About everybody's prints being in IAFIS."

"Who knows? They could be. The NSA reads our e-mails, why not take our prints, too?"

She was quiet a moment before she said, "I read about you. Kai told me I should read up on you a little. About how your partner almost killed you. Eli Sherman. I remember the news coming out about him, that a homicide detective was a serial killer. I was still at the academy. I wondered what that would do to his partner. How he must've felt knowing the person watching his back was the monster he was looking for."

Stanton stared at the pavement. At the mention of his former partner's name, it all came rushing back to him as though it had just occurred. He was shot at Sherman's house, flipped over the banister, and impacting with the floor. He had to crawl to his weapon, which was casually hanging in its holster slung over one of Sherman's dining room chairs. Stanton hadn't seen it. He had been completely fooled. Sherman had come to his home for Sunday dinners, spent time with his children, and taken them to Padres baseball games... Stanton had been so blinded that until the moment the hot slug entered his flesh, he hadn't believed Sherman was capable of such great evil.

"Didn't feel good," he said quietly.

"I bet. But that's what life is, right? A big learning experience."

Stanton didn't move or blink. His eyes were fixed on a scrap of paper rustling in the breeze away from the hotel's entrance. "Didn't feel like much of a learning experience. Other than teaching me that anyone is capable of anything." He looked at her. "Where were you before Homicide?"

"Vice."

Stanton nodded. It made sense. Young, attractive officers were routinely recruited to the vice squad across departments to be used in prostitution and illegal pornography stings. "Why did you want to do this?"

"Homicide? Other than a pay bump? It's got everything I became a cop for. My dad was a cop, Kai's brother. That's how Kai got into it after he blew out his knee and couldn't play football anymore. So it was never really a question for me. My dad was here twenty years ago. Then my uncle. Now me."

"Just following in your family's footsteps? I don't buy it. That gets you only so far. You have to want to transfer here. You specifically asked for Homicide."

"I think I can do some good. And I was sick of dressing in miniskirts and heels."

He grinned. "Whatever the reason, make sure you remember it. Write it down somewhere. Because you'll forget. The weight of it will start suffocating you. If you write down why you're here, you can read it and keep going."

"Why are you here?"

Stanton paused. Then he dipped his fingers into his breast pocket and pulled out a small laminated card about the size of a business card. He handed it to her, and she read it.

"Know that God loves us and remember that if you stare too long into the abyss, the abyss will stare back into you," she said aloud. "Huh."

"It's what keeps me going. And it's a warning. Our brains are very much like computers. Garbage in, garbage out. You're going to see things you didn't think possible. So you have to remember those two things." She went to hand the card back to him, and he said, "Keep it. I have more. Keep it in your pocket whenever you start your shift. Just like your gun and badge."

"Thanks."

Stanton glanced over at Russell. He was nervously pacing back and forth. He wasn't a psychopath, Stanton guessed. Most psychopaths displayed neither stress nor surprise.

One famous study by a psychologist in the Midwest was a subject of controversy because the results were so against the paradigms then held in academic psychology. The examiner would shock the subject after counting down from ten. The subjects were hooked up to stress machines to monitor perspiration, heart rate, blood pressure, *et cetera*. Normal, non-psychopaths' stress levels skyrocketed when the examiner got close to one. The psychopaths had no such reactions. Their stress levels stayed level even during the shock.

Russell appeared agitated and on the brink of an anxiety attack. Something unanticipated had occurred, and he'd reacted with extreme anger. When he'd calmed, he probably regretted the decision but chose not to call the police.

"Let's go," Stanton said. He turned on the digital recorder he always kept with him while he was on duty and slipped it into his breast pocket.

The two of them walked over to Russell, and Stanton stood in front of him. He didn't say anything for a moment, just held the man's eyes, which were wide and full of fear.

"You know what I'm going to say, don't you, Russell?"

He opened his mouth to say something then stopped, opting instead to just nod. Finally, he answered, "You found my DNA on the statue."

Stanton nodded. "Why would you think you could get away with this? You're not a killer, Russell."

"I know," he said, his voice shaky and his eyes glistening. "I know I'm not. I didn't want to hurt him. I really didn't. I loved him. I would never hurt him. But he… he slept with someone else. I paid for this whole vacation. I pay all his bills, let him stay at my house, buy his food… pay his car insurance. And so I get to go on one vacation a year, and he fucks someone else. Don't even tell me you wouldn't wig out, too."

"You had a right to be upset. I'm not denying that. I haven't seen the statue, and they didn't describe it to me. What was it?"

He put his hands over his face, rubbing furiously. "Just some native thing. Like a totem pole or something."

"Like a Tiki totem?"

"Yeah, I guess. I don't know."

"The SIS unit didn't tell me where they found it. Was it in the trash at the hotel?"

"No… no, I hid it in the plant by the ice machine. Shit. Shit, shit, shit."

Stanton glanced back to Laka, who nodded and ran into the hotel, grabbing one of the forensic techs on her way. Stanton turned back to Russell just as he began to cry. Stanton placed his hand on his shoulder. Though a murderer, he was still a human being. And Stanton had always had a difficult time seeing people, any people, in pain.

"Take a minute, Russell. And then you and I have to go on a ride."

His hand on Russell's shoulder, Stanton stood next to the man while he wept.

7

By the time Stanton had taken an official statement from Russell Neal, it was nearly midnight. Russell had gone through the murder in detail. He'd found out his boyfriend was cheating, confronted him, grabbed the Tiki totem, and struck him over the head with it. The uniforms found the totem where Russell had said it was going to be— in a vase holding a bamboo plant near the elevators on his floor.

At some point, Russell would find out Stanton had lied about finding the totem, but it didn't matter. The United States Supreme Court had long held that deception was an acceptable interrogation tactic. But a slight twinge of remorse still worked its way through Stanton, like a worm crawling over a slick surface. He knew, logically, he shouldn't feel any remorse because the greater evil would be punished, but he couldn't help it.

Laka had been in the interrogation room with him the entire time. She'd never postured, yawned, or complained. She just sat quietly and observed. When they were through, she followed him to the bullpen and sat in a chair next to his desk.

"That was much more interesting than I thought it was going to be," she said. "Do most murders close that quickly?"

"If within forty-eight hours, you don't have a good idea of who your collar's going to be, the case is unlikely to be solved. Most of the time, you know who you're going to arrest in those first two days, and you're right ninety percent of the time."

She smirked. "But not you?"

"What'd you mean?"

"I saw the articles about you. That you're psychic and all that. You don't close all your cases in forty-eight hours."

"If they're going to be closed, most of mine close within the first forty-eight. It's like that for every cop in every city. There's either witnesses that tell you who did it, they feel guilty and turn themselves in, or they leave so much evidence behind that it's like a sign pointing directly to them. The ones that don't have those things are the ones likely to get away with it. At least for a while."

"The ones you specialize in? That's what Kai told me. That you specialize in the cases everyone else gives up on."

"I don't know about 'specialize,' but they certainly give them to me."

She grinned and brushed aside a strand of hair from her face. For the first time in a long time, Stanton's heart fluttered. He turned away from her.

"Get some sleep. We'll do the report writing in the morning."

"Thanks."

He pretended to be doing something on the computer as she rose. But she didn't leave. Laka stood there until Stanton looked at her.

"Thanks. A lot of cops, when they get a more inexperienced partner, aren't exactly nice to them right off the bat."

She smiled and turned to walk away. Stanton watched her for a moment then faced his computer again. He told himself she was too young and that she didn't deserve to be with someone who had a relationship track record like his. He was incapable of forming that deep connection with everyone except one woman… who had turned out to be psychotic.

Stanton rose and walked outside. The air was warm as he stood on the sidewalk, looking at the palace across the street. In the dark, it looked much larger than it was. He could imagine enemy tribes attacking and being awed by its size and fortifications.

Stanton walked casually to his Jeep and drove to a grocery store. He picked up a few bags of sandwiches, sodas, and chips. Honolulu's red-light district wasn't far from the precinct, and he drove there slowly, listening to a Joy Division album he'd purchased recently, a collection of rare B-sides.

The district was really nothing more than alleyways and main intersections where the girls hung out and showed off what they had with revealing clothing. The mix of prostitutes never ceased to amaze him. Young girls all the way up to the elderly strutted the sidewalks. And the police presence was practically nonexistent.

Stanton parked and got out. Groups of women approached him. Since arriving in Hawaii, he had been coming there to drop off food. Some of the women worked forty or fifty hours straight without a single thing to eat or drink. Stanton dropped off food on the odd Friday or Saturday night, and he never had anything left over.

Some of the girls thanked him, and others didn't make eye contact. Many had experienced lifetimes of betrayal at the hands of the people they trusted most, and they eyed Stanton suspiciously. A few of the girls had even told him they wouldn't eat his food for fear of it being poisoned. He often heard them whispering among themselves that he had to be nuts to do what he did.

When the food was gone, Stanton climbed back into the Jeep. One girl, who was perhaps sixteen or seventeen, leaned into the Jeep and asked, "So did you want a freebie?"

"No, I wouldn't do that." He turned on the engine. "I haven't seen you out here before."

"Nah, I'm new. Just got here from San Francisco. So you with the shelter or somethin'?"

"No, I'm not with them. How old are you?"

"Eighteen."

"Eighteen or sixteen?"

She hesitated. "I can be whatever the perverts out here want me to be."

Stanton glanced down at his phone. It was ringing, a number from the precinct. He let the call go to voicemail.

"What's your name?" he asked.

"Mindy."

"Mindy, you see those women right there? Right on the corner? That one in the skirt is fifty-six years old. Her name's Rachel. She's been doing this for forty years. She got started at fifteen and has been on the street ever since."

"I got a dad," she said, stepping away from the Jeep.

"No, I'm not lecturing you. If you want to be like her, that's your choice. You have free will to become who you want to become. But what you put out into the world is exactly what you get back. If you don't want to be like her, I know someone that can help."

She tucked a strand of hair behind her ear. "Who?"

Stanton took out one of his cards. It had his cell number and e-mail address on it. He handed it to her. "Call me in the morning, and I'll get you set up with her. She's a social worker that helps girls just like you get off the street. She can set you up with an apartment and a job or finishing school if you don't have a diploma."

The girl took the card. "You're a cop?"

"Yes." Stanton saw one of the older women get into a sedan, which drove off. "How much do you make a night out here?"

"Good night? Two hundred. Tonight'll be slow, though, 'cause of the football game. Johns will be with their families and stuff."

Stanton took out his wallet. He only had eighty in cash. "This is all the cash I have. It's for tonight. I'm buying your night. Go stay in a motel and call me as soon as you wake up. Okay?"

She stared at the card then tucked it into her bra. "Okay."

Stanton watched the girl march down the sidewalk and disappear from view. He'd delivered that card and pitch before, at least fifty times. As far as he could remember, only three girls had ever taken him up on it.

He put his Jeep in drive and pulled away from the curb.

Stanton took a long drive up the shore. Insomnia had plagued him recently. Actually, it plagued him constantly. He couldn't recall a single night, even when he was a teenager, when he'd slept soundly and woken up refreshed. Nightmares and memories better left forgotten always haunted him. Fragments of sensations about other people often hit him in the middle of the night, and he could never get back to sleep.

A San Diego homicide case stuck out for him. A woman had been hacked to pieces in her apartment. The window was broken out, and everyone had assumed it was a home invasion turned murder. But something didn't sit right with the way the victim was displayed.

Her entire body had been mutilated and torn apart… except her head. That had been covered with a sheet. That night, Stanton was deep in sleep when he saw the murder. Later, he told himself he'd merely seen his own interpretation, but while the dream was occurring, he could've sworn he was witnessing the actual thing.

The man who'd cut her up couldn't look at her face. Every time he saw it, guilt unleashed itself inside him, and he would have to stop. So he covered her head with a sheet and dealt only with the body. After he was done, he broke out the window to make it seem like a home invasion.

One of the officers at the scene couldn't look at the head once the sheet was gone. A dead body, even to those with lots of experience with them, was an odd thing. Stanton had seen coroners poke and prod corpses like a curious boy with a stick when they thought no one was looking. But the officer wouldn't even turn in the direction of the head.

When Stanton arrived on the officer's doorstep for nothing more than to chat about the murder, the officer somehow just knew that Stanton knew. They'd held each other's gaze for a long time before the officer broke into a run and escaped through a bathroom window. A squad car picked him up down the block from his home. Inside a drawer in his bedroom was a ring from the victim.

Those sensations—"leaps," as one of his former bosses, Michael Harlow, had called them—came to him in quiet moments, such as when he was left alone at a crime scene, asleep, or taking a warm bath in the candlelight. He had always told people that he just looked at the evidence and that everyone was capable of coming to the conclusions he came to. But after the case with the police officer, he wasn't sure.

Stanton headed home. His house, a spacious two-story of glass and white carpet he'd bought with his much-wealthier fiancée at the time, was dark and empty. He threw his keys in a bowl on the dining room table then flopped on the couch. Though every muscle, sinew, and bone screamed to him that he was fatigued and needed sleep, he knew sleep wouldn't come. Too much mental energy was built up in his mind. Surfing, jogging, and working cases released that energy. And he hadn't done enough of those that day.

He flipped on the television. The blue light flickered in the dark, but he wasn't paying attention. His mind was a million miles away.

8

Morning came quickly. Sharon hadn't come home, nothing that she hadn't done a thousand times before. Usually, it meant a decent night's sleep for him... but something was different. He had been guzzling Pepto-Bismol the past few days. When his stomach wasn't gurgling, it was sour or gassy. All in all, he felt as though he had the stomach flu without all the symptoms.

As he rose from bed and let the sunshine into his bedroom by pulling up the blinds, he thought he should visit the doctor. Maybe he had caught a little bug. In general, he'd felt lousy all week.

Richard took his phone off the nightstand and checked for text messages. Sharon had a yoga class the night before, but he hadn't received any information from Tate. It apparently hadn't happened then. *No big deal,* he thought. They were probably just really thorough.

After a quick breakfast, he showered and shaved. Then he went into Eliza's bedroom. She was still asleep, though it was eight o'clock.

"Sweetie, time to get up."

"Okay, daddy, one minute."

"No, not one minute, now."

She groaned and threw back the cover. "This sucks."

"School or waking up?"

"Both."

"Well, get used to it, 'cause going to work every morning is even worse."

Richard waited until Eliza had dressed and then made her egg whites with a Diet Coke, her preferred breakfast. As his daughter ate in front of him at the table, he just watched her. When she was younger, he'd watched her sleep or play outside. He didn't get to do that much anymore.

"Big plans today?" he asked.

She shook her head. "School and then Cheer. You?"

"Just work."

"Sounds fun." She paused. "Where's Mom?"

He cleared his throat and wiped pretend crumbs from the table. "She's on a business trip."

"Business trip again, huh? She goes on a lot of business trips for someone that doesn't have a job."

"It's just the way of things."

"Dad, cut it out."

"Cut what out?" he said, grinning.

"I'm not a little kid anymore. I know she has boyfriends."

His grin disappeared. "You do, do you?"

"Why haven't you divorced her?"

"Now you just hold on a minute. That's your mother. You don't say things like that about your mother."

"What? That I want you two to divorce? Why not? I think you deserve someone better than her. She's a shitty mom and a shittier wife."

"Now hold on just a dang minute, Eliza. You do not talk about your mother that way. Do you know what I would do to spend even a day with my mother again? When she passed, a part of me went with her. You don't see it now, but that's how it'll be with your mother, too. You only get one."

"Thankfully. I couldn't handle two of her," she mumbled under her breath.

A car horn, no doubt belonging to another carpool parent, blared in the street. Eliza jumped up and said, "I'll see you, Daddy." She kissed his cheek.

"See you, honey."

When she was gone, Richard sat at the table alone and looked out the window over the sink. He'd sat there alone many, many times and thought about that very topic. Everything Eliza had said was true. Sharon was a terrible mother and wife. She wasn't just terrible. Many parents were neglectful, but Sharon was something else. She was... malicious, as though she wanted to hurt Richard and Eliza with her actions.

Richard sighed and rose to clear away the dishes before heading out to his car. The Cadillac was new and still had that clean leather smell. He soaked it in on the drive to his office as he listened to the oldies station. "Good Vibrations" by the Beach Boys was playing, one of his favorites. He'd actually seen the Beach Boys live once in the seventies. It had been one of his first, and he remembered everything about the concert. The smell of the crowd, all packed tightly together in that arena. The lights bouncing off the walls and ceilings. The music reverberating through the floors and into his feet. He'd been so poor at the time that he'd had to skip several meals that month to pay for the concert ticket. Very poor and very happy.

The office was buzzing with activity. Paralegals were filing things, receptionists were busy on the phones, and several attorneys were in the conference room for a partners meeting. As Richard walked past the glass conference room, he stopped. He should have been one of the firm's eight partners. He'd been there longer than anyone but the founding partners, and he billed a hell of a lot more than even they did. Tax and estates was a thriving field as the baby boomers retired.

The meeting appeared to be coming to a close, and the partners rose and began filing out. The senior partner, Candice Strain, stayed behind to look through documents. Richard nodded hello to some of the partners, and they acknowledged him but didn't say anything back as they scurried to their offices.

He opened the conference room door. Candice didn't notice him as he entered, so he cleared his throat. She looked up, and he smiled awkwardly.

"Hi."

"What can I do for you, Richard?"

"Um, well, I was just… You know, I've been here a long time, Candice. I mean, I came on a year after you founded the place. And, well, I've seen a lot of younger guys make partner ahead of me. And I've held my tongue because I know you know what you're doing, but I was thinking that—"

"Get to the point, Richard. My time is limited."

"I deserve to be a partner."

She lowered the papers. Leaning back in the leather chair, she looked like an ancient queen about to pass judgment on one of her serfs. "Richard, I couldn't do what I do if I didn't have people like you. I may sign the clients up, but they stay because of the quality of work people like you do in the back offices."

"People like me?"

"Yes, Richard, people like you."

He shifted his weight from one foot to the other, uncertain what to do with his hands. "People like me who never become a partner, you mean."

"You're a brilliant lawyer. But a partner has nothing to do with being a brilliant lawyer. I can hire brilliant lawyers. I don't need to be brilliant. I need to know how to sell. You can't sell the clients, Richard."

"Sure I can. Mrs. Dillar is one of our biggest clients, and when she calls, she only talks to me."

"I know. But she wouldn't have come to this firm if you had been the one to meet with her first. That's not your strength, Richard. We all have to go with our strengths. And yours is right where you are."

He nodded, staring down at the floor. "Thanks for your time."

As he shuffled out of the office, three of the paralegals, all attractive, passed by. He smiled, but they didn't smile back.

Richard shut the door to his office and put his feet up on the desk. He didn't move for a long time. The outside walls were just windows, and he could see the streets of Honolulu below him. Fancy cars passed by, and the women who walked the streets could've been pulled from any *Playboy* he'd ever seen.

He took out his cell phone and dialed the number he'd been given.

"Yeah," Tate Reynolds answered.

"She had yoga last night. Why isn't this done yet?"

"Hey, calm down. You want it done right, or you want it done fast?"

"I want it done both. It needs to get done." Richard noticed his voice was louder than he would've liked. Taking his feet off the desk, he tried to calm himself. "When?"

"Tonight."

"You sure? It's really tonight?"

"Yes."

He rose and paced his office. "I mean, if you need more time, then take it. I didn't mean to rush you."

"Tonight's as good as any. We'll do it tonight."

"All right... all right."

"So you cool?"

"Yeah," Richard said. "Yeah, I'm cool."

"Good."

Richard waited for Tate to hang up first, then he placed the phone down on his desk. He was chewing on his thumbnail and pacing manically around his office when the door opened.

"Richard?" Candice stood in the doorway, leaning against the door.

"Yeah."

"You okay?"

"Just dandy. Why?"

"I felt bad about that conversation. I think I could've handled that more delicately, and I'm sorry."

"I appreciate that." He didn't know where to put his hands, so he put them on his hips, but that felt awkward, so he put them in his pockets. That didn't feel right, either, so he took them out and let them dangle at his sides.

"Yes, well, how about this? We'll give you a nice little bonus this quarter and an extra week of vacation time. Take your family to Europe or something."

"Yeah, sure, listen, I just kinda need to be alone right now."

"Okay, but I want you to know that you're valued here."

"Right, valued." He began to pace again.

"Well, what I'm trying to say is—"

"Candice, for fuck's sake, I said I wanted to be alone. Damn it, what the hell do I have to do to get some quiet here?"

Candice said nothing. Slowly, she shut the door, leaving Richard alone again. He sighed and ran his hands through his hair. He approached the door to find her and apologize then stopped himself. It wouldn't help.

He grunted and swiped at his desk, knocking his lamp to the floor. Then he stared at the ceiling and let out a big breath. He left the lamp where it was and decided he needed to get a stiff drink. He had a feeling he would be counting down the seconds until nine o'clock, when Sharon's yoga class let out.

9

Stanton woke in the morning and went immediately for a run. He preferred running barefoot because the natural stride was easy on his knees and ankles. The North Shore was ideal for it. The sand wasn't too soft, but it gave enough that he could zone out and watch the ocean, letting whatever thoughts naturally come to him take hold in his mind.

The sun was just coming up over the Pacific, painting it light gold then crimson. Flocks of birds hovered above the waves, and farther out, blue fish darted in and out of the water.

The run was smooth and easy. Stanton got in four miles before he stopped and checked his heart rate. Then he sat on the beach and watched the sunrise. Groups of young surfers were out. They had no jobs and devoted their lives to the ocean. Most would move on to other things. But some of them would stay because detaching themselves from the sea would be their death. They would become the middle-aged men Stanton saw on the beaches six hours a day and then later at the beach parties and weekend bonfires. They could never quite break away.

He rose and strolled back to his house, watching the surfers glide ashore. The waves were mushy and slow. He wouldn't be going out that day unless they picked up around evening.

When he got back to his house, a car was out front. Laka sat inside, texting. She looked up at him and smiled.

"Hi," she said, stepping out.

"Hey. What're you doing here?"

"I thought I'd pick you up."

"I appreciate it, but I've got my own car."

She seemed almost hurt. Stanton often forgot how young some people were. And that with youth came a sense that everyone, somehow, had to like you and want to spend time with you. "But since you're here, lemme hit the shower, and then we'll head in."

Stanton led her inside his home. He went to the kitchen for some water and noticed her examining his house—she even looked over his DVD collection.

"Interesting movie selection," she said.

Stanton guzzled a glass of ice water. "They're mostly my sons' movies."

"Oh? I didn't know you had sons. How many?"

"Two."

"They live here?"

"No, they live with their mother in Boston. But they lived here for a year before moving back."

She picked up a framed photo of his two boys. "My parents divorced when I was a kid, too. They went one step further, though, and told me I had to choose who to live with. They wouldn't do it for me."

Stanton leaned against the island in the kitchen. "Who'd you pick?"

"My dad. My mom remarried, had other kids. By the time I was fifteen, I only got a card on my birthday from her. But my dad's always been there."

"He lives on the island?"

"Yeah. I'll have to introduce you to him. He makes the best Huli-Huli chicken you'll ever have."

Stanton placed his water glass by the sink. "Why did Kai really partner us, Laka? There are far better detectives than me to show you the ropes."

"I don't know. Before I even transferred, he said he wanted me with you."

Stanton watched her a moment, taking in the way she moved. He hadn't had a woman in his house for so long, he had forgotten what it felt like. "I better go hit the shower."

Stanton stripped off his clothing once he was on the second floor and threw them into a laundry bin. The water heated up instantly, and he let it run over his head and down his back. He kept thinking of Laka. She was exotically beautiful. Her straight hair was inky black, and her skin appeared so smooth that she didn't need makeup. Stanton had to stop his thoughts, though. She was his partner, and there was no surer path to destroying a career and partnership than starting up a relationship. If it didn't work out, one of them would have to request a new partner and maybe even transfer from Homicide.

He toweled off and put on jeans, a button-down shirt, and a leather jacket. Laka was sitting on his balcony, watching the ocean.

"This is why I bought this place," he said.

"I always take it for granted. Growing up on the islands, you forget about it." She took a deep breath and rose. "Ready?"

"Yeah."

Stanton sat in the passenger seat, and Laka drove. The car was immaculately clean, to the point that it didn't appear to have even been driven before. Hanging from her rearview mirror was a framed painting no bigger than a few inches wide, depicting Jesus and his twelve apostles.

H1 was practically empty that morning, and they zipped down the interstate. Stanton kept his window down and his eyes fixed on the passing landscape, but they occasionally drifted over to the beautiful woman sitting next to him. The acute pain of loneliness was never greater than when he was with someone else.

"I read some stuff," she said, "about you."

"Kai tell you to do that?"

"No. I looked it up on my own. About how you testified against your former chief for corruption charges. That couldn't have been easy."

"No, it certainly wasn't. Mike was my friend, as well as being my boss."

"Then why'd you do it? Most cops wouldn't have."

"I think every choice we make leads to one of two things. Either chaos or order. I can't choose chaos. There's so much of that already that I'm not sure we'll ever have order. But I can't contribute to it."

"So you think every choice is going to lead to that?"

"Yes. That's the only choice we really have. Do you want chaos? Or do you want order? Nothing else really matters."

Laka pulled to a stop in front of the station, and an ambulance was there. Two EMTs were talking in front of the station. Farther off was a fire truck.

"What's going on?" Laka asked.

"I don't know."

Stanton hurried inside. The din that normally accompanied his first steps into the precinct was there, but something was off. Some people were talking in hushed tones, and a few stared as he walked by. Stanton rode the elevator to the fifth floor, where Kai was speaking with two paramedics. He waited until they were finished then went to Kai.

"What's going on?" Stanton asked.

Kai's brow furrowed like a bulldog's. "Come into my office, bra." Kai shut the door as Stanton sat down. Kai settled into his seat and took a sip of a fruity drink before placing his hands on the desk. "You got that confession last night. That was good work. Russell Neal. That's exactly how I want you to work these cases. And nothing that happens after is in our control. We just make the collars and move to the next case."

"What happened?" Stanton asked. But the sinking feeling in his stomach already told him.

"Mr. Neal decided to take his own life… after he found out that we hadn't found the murder weapon when he'd confessed. Jon, we know each other a long time, bra. Have I ever been anything but straight with you?"

"No."

"Then believe me when I say this ain't your fault. Nothin' you could've done would've stopped this."

Stanton nodded. "I appreciate you telling me." He stood. "Anything else?"

"No." He leaned back in his chair. "That's it."

When Stanton left the office, Laka was waiting for him by the bullpen, but he didn't go there. He marched straight toward the elevator and pushed the button. When it took too long, he opted to take the stairs.

Though he meant to keep an even pace down the five flights, he found himself nearly running. He burst out into the warm air. He needed to get out of there, away from everyone. His chest felt tight, and his vision blurred. He was sucking breath as if he were facedown in sand. Though the world spun, he dashed for the palace across the street. A car horn blasted somewhere near him. A moment later, he felt the soft grass underneath his shoes. He leaned against a tree and slid to the ground, sweat beginning to sting his eyes.

# 10

Tate Reynolds sat in the RV in a grocery store parking lot, smoking a cigarette laced with angel dust. Much better than anything else he'd ever taken, it gave him confidence, energy, and power—things he constantly craved.

Hiapo and the third man, an emaciated guy everyone called Sticks, were inside the grocery store. Tate had told them to get sandwiches and chips, but he knew they would come back with mostly beer. They were still kids, young punks just drifting around until they got pinched again. Hiapo had done a good stretch of three to ten before, but Sticks had only spent a week inside here and there. That made Tate nervous. He'd been in just long enough to be scared but not used to being inside. Sticks might flip if the cops applied pressure.

The RV door opened, and Hiapo waddled in and laid a sack on the kitchen counter. The RV, as a whole, was the nicest vehicle Tate had ever been in. This Richard really didn't fuck around when it came to spending cash.

"Did you get sandwiches?" Tate asked.

"A few. You want a beer?"

"No, I don't want a beer, dumbass. If I wanted beer, I would have told you to get beer. I wanted sandwiches."

"Calm down. I got you a sandwich."

Hiapo handed him a foot-long sub. Tate unwrapped the Saran wrap and took a bite. The bread was stale, and the mayonnaise, warm. But he'd had far worse.

"There she is," Hiapo said.

Tate looked up to see a woman in spandex pants and a tank top walk out of the grocery store. The muscles in her arms and chest were visible, but her boobs were huge, clearly fake. Her blond hair was bright, almost platinum, and her nails were painted black.

"Holy shit," Sticks said. "She's fucking hot."

Tate took another bite of the sandwich. "Shit," he mumbled.

"You sure we gotta do this?" Hiapo asked.

"What? She gives you a woody, and you can't off her now?"

"Nah, I mean, woman like that. Ya know. Husband might pay more than we're gettin' to get her back. Ya know."

Tate placed the sandwich down and picked up his cigarette. "That idea ain't total shit. But I bet some people might pay more for a piece of ass like that." He pulled out his cell phone and dialed a man named Lee.

"Yo," Lee said. "What's up, brother?"

"Chillin'. Hey, you still know Marvin up there in the docks?"

"Yeah, why?"

"He still into girls?"

"Girls?"

"Yeah, dipshit. He still buyin' girls?"

"Shit, I don't know. I ain't seen him for a minute."

"Do me a solid—go see him. Ask him if he still got the hook-up on buyin' bitches. I got a fine one for him."

"A'ight, I'll check and hit you up."

Tate placed the phone down on the dash. Sharon Miller got into her car and fiddled with her stereo before pulling away. Tate started the RV and followed.

11

Stanton sat in Dr. Vaquer's waiting room. He was hunched over, staring at the floor, when her doors opened and she said, "Please come in."

He rose and followed her inside. The office was always the same, not a painting or stapler out of place. Some psychiatrists used the method to offer their patients consistency.

He sat down on the couch and leaned back. The ceiling fan wasn't on. Instead, the window was open, and Stanton could hear the traffic outside. Dr. Vaquer must've noticed, because she rose and closed the window before sitting back down across from him.

"Tell me about the attack," she said.

"My chest started feeling tight. Then my vision was affected. It was like I was looking through a rolled-up piece of paper or something. Myopic. I kept blinking to make it go away like it was something in my eye. Then my thoughts jumbled, and my chest felt like it might burst open from the pressure. I passed out, but luckily, I was leaning against a tree. When I woke up, I think a couple of minutes had passed. But I don't know for sure."

She stared at him a moment. "Was there something unusual or particularly stressful that you feel triggered it?"

"A collar I had on a murder. He grabbed a gun from the officer guarding him when he went in to feed him. He shot himself. I got a confession out of him by lying to him that we'd found the murder weapon. When he found out that wasn't true, he killed himself."

She nodded. "Jon, I'm very worried about this attack. You haven't had a panic attack in over a year. And this one sounds particularly worrisome because you fainted."

"I know."

"I'd like to put you on another medication. Xanax. It should help with these attacks."

He shook his head. "I'm fine. They're rare enough that they don't interfere."

"I won't contradict your wishes, of course, but that's the wrong choice. It's okay to need help sometimes."

He was silent for a while. "I've been having nightmares again."

"What of?"

"Last night, I saw myself in a car. It was a luxury car, a Mercedes or something. I was driving it for someone else. They had asked me to take it somewhere. The road was really dark. All I could see were the lines speeding past me and darkness everywhere else. The car kept going faster and faster, so I put my foot on the brake, but it didn't work. This red circle came on in the dash—a warning light that isn't actually on a dashboard. I didn't know what it was. I called the Mercedes dealership, but no one answered."

"What do you think it means?"

"I don't know, but when I woke up, my pillow was soaked. I thought it was sweat at first, but I wasn't sweating. I was crying."

"You were weeping in your sleep?"

He nodded. "I've never done that before."

She considered that a moment then said, "Jon, this is very important. I would like to put you on Xanax to control the anxiety attacks. And I'd like to increase the dosage for the Prozac."

He shook his head. "Medication isn't the answer."

"Then what is?"

"There's something... I don't know. It feels like I'm being told something."

She placed her hands together, casually rubbing them before leaning back in her seat and crossing her legs. "We've talked about this before. Your belief in visions. I know you have a very powerful belief in God. Do you believe God gives you visions?"

"Yes."

"Is it just because of your Mormon faith, or do you think there are deeper reasons?"

"No, there's deeper reasons."

"Like what?"

Stanton paused. "I've had them before."

"Tell me about one."

"They're just fragments. Impressions, almost. When I was in Sex Crimes, we found some remains we couldn't identify in an abandoned building. The most accurate way to identify a body is with dental records. Everything else fades with time and exposure to the environment. But this vic was missing all their teeth. So identification was almost impossible." He swallowed and paused a moment. "One night, after we had already closed the case and transferred it to the Open-Unsolved files, I saw something in a dream. A young girl standing in a dress and high heels. Her hair was cut short, and her nose and cheeks were rosy, like she'd been exposed to a lot of wind or something. Her hands were up, blocking something coming toward her. And her eyes… they looked more terrified than any eyes I've ever seen. She knew she was going to die.

"But she was standing still. And I couldn't figure out why she wasn't running… until it hit me that it was a photo. There was a photo of her somewhere. A photo of the vic before she was killed." He was quiet a long time but didn't look Dr. Vaquer in the eyes. "A few months later, a trucker named Randy Gomez was arrested by the FBI for an unrelated case. But his home was in San Diego, so we were brought in on the search. They found a photograph of a young girl in an abandoned building. It was tucked underneath his pillow. She was in heels, her hands were up defending her, and the look on her face was…"

"Was it her?"

"Identical to what I saw in my dream. He confessed to killing her."

Neither of them spoke or moved. Stanton exhaled loudly. "Can we talk about something else?"

12

The RV had a smooth ride, but it was hard to hide in traffic. Tate wished he'd thought about that before following Sharon Miller. But she didn't seem like the kind of lady who would be constantly looking in her rearview mirror anyway.

They crossed the island, Tate always staying as far back as he could without losing her. Eventually, they reached a neighborhood Tate had never been to, with large houses with immense lawns and swimming pools in the back. Shiny luxury cars were in every driveway. When he was a kid, Tate always pictured himself living in a place like that. But life had taken him another direction. He still had the desire to live there, but not the means to make it happen.

Sharon parked in a driveway, went to the door, and knocked. The man who answered kissed her, his hands drifting down to her ass. She went inside, and the door shut behind her.

"Shit," Hiapo said. "She's scandalous. Guess all bitches are."

Tate turned off the RV and took out a joint from a small plastic baggie on the floor. He lit up and took a few puffs before handing it to Hiapo, who was in the passenger seat. "You had a mama. Was your mama scandalous?"

"No," Hiapo said, inhaling from the joint.

"Then not all bitches are scandalous, are they?"

Sticks came up front, having just woken from his nap on the bed in the back of the RV. He was rubbing his eyes when he took the joint from Hiapo. He inhaled a big pull and held it.

"What we doing?" he asked in that high-pitched squeal stoners got when holding in smoke.

"She's with some dude," Tate said.

"Good. Just walk up and bust a cap in her, man."

"Fuck no. They got gunshot residue and DNA and all that shit, man. I ain't riskin' goin' back inside."

"So what you wanna do?" he asked, exhaling smoke.

"We gonna take her in the RV and dump her somewhere in the ocean. Let the sharks have her, man. No body, no murder. That's what this fucker in the can used to say to me. Said he killed, like, ten girls and got rid of all the bodies, so he was only in there for a robbery."

"No body, huh?" Sticks pulled the joint away and hungrily took a few more puffs.

"We got a Playstation back there. Just hang out, man."


Several hours passed. Tate smoked so much weed that he felt slow and bloated… and hungry. But the dumb bastards had only picked up two sandwiches, which were already gone. He rose and carefully walked to the fridge. He opened it to find two six-packs of beer. At least it was something. He grabbed a bottle and returned to the driver's seat. The beer was warm since the fridge wasn't on.

"Hey," Hiapo said, "There she is."

Sharon Miller stepped out of the house, and the man at the door watched her for a while. She got into her car, blew him a kiss, then pulled out. Tate ducked low in the seat and waited a few minutes before turning on the RV and following.

She seemed to be rocketing away from them, although she was probably just going the speed limit. Tate did his best to keep up, but he was so high that he was anxious whenever he hit forty miles an hour.

"Shit," he said. "I'm too fucking high."

"Let me drive," Hiapo said.

Tate slid out and collapsed into the passenger seat as Hiapo took his place. Tate closed his eyes then felt sick, so he opened them and rolled down the window. Warm air hit his face as the RV sped onto the freeway, and he thought he might vomit.

They seemed to drive forever before arriving at a mall. They followed the car around and parked in a wide-open space. Sharon got out and hustled into the mall.

"I'm fucking sick," Tate said, opening the door.

"Where you going?" Sticks asked from the back.

"I don't know. Food court. Get some Sprite or something."

"Get me a Big Mac and some fries."

"Fuck you. Get it yourself."

"Don't be a bitch. Just get it."

Tate stumbled out, squinting in the harsh light. He reached into the RV for his sunglasses then flipped them on. The mall was large and flat. The largest mall in Honolulu, most of it was outdoors under a retractable cover. He stumbled through the parking lot and opened the doors. The food court was right inside. He staggered around until he saw a McDonald's.

The line moved so slowly that he started counting the tiles on the floor. The next door didn't have a line, so he strolled over there and leaned against the counter, staring at the menu. When he felt somebody behind him, he glanced back and saw Sharon Miller standing there.

He snapped his head forward as the cashier came up to him. "What can I get for you?"

Tate looked at the first thing on the menu. "Um, a turkey and cheese and a Sprite."

The clerk continued asking questions, and Tate answered, but he kept glancing behind him. Sharon was on the phone. She was, he decided, much hotter up close. His chest felt tight, and he was starting to sweat. He turned and marched out of the food court without getting his sandwich or drink, the cashier shouting behind him.

13

Several hours later, Tate was finally sober enough to drive. Sharon Miller spent the entire day shopping. By the time night fell, the RV was the last place any of the men wanted to be. It stank of weed, farts, and beer.

Tate leaned his head against the glass and let out a loud belch. His eyes shut, and he felt himself drifting off. Sticks had been passed out for a while, and Hiapo was doing something on his phone.

Tate felt a hand on his shoulder and jolted awake. He hadn't realized he'd been sleeping. Hiapo stood over him. "She's out."

Hiapo took the driver's seat, and the RV roared to life. It followed the car onto the freeway then headed back downtown. After a few minutes, they were in an upscale neighborhood a lot like the one they'd been to before. Then Sharon opened a garage and pulled her car in.

"Shit," Hiapo said. "This is her house."

Tate shrugged. "Let's go, then."

He walked to the back of the RV and kicked Sticks. The man snored louder and turned over. Tate pushed his head into the pillow until he started struggling and kicking his legs.

"Get up, dipshit. We're here."

Tate pulled out a bag he'd brought as a back-up plan. Richard had wanted him to kidnap his wife, take her to an RV park, and kill her there. The RV wouldn't have been bothered for a long time, and the body would have just been sitting there, decomposing until someone noticed the smell. But dumping her in the ocean would be easier. Less messy. And the cops would probably never find it.

Tate took out three ski masks and tossed one to each man. He was the first one out of the RV, and he didn't wait for the other two. Sneaking through the bushes, he slid along the garage and knocked on the door. The neighborhood was dark, but it was possible the neighbors could see them. He needed to work quickly.

He heard the lock unfasten, and a young girl opened the door. She tried to scream, but Tate rushed her. He slapped his palm over her mouth, muffling her scream, and picked her up off her feet as he pushed the door open and stomped inside. Hiapo and Sticks followed him.

Tate pinned the girl onto the floor. "Watch her," he told the other two.

Hiapo placed his foot on the girl's chest, but he didn't hold her mouth. He just said, "Shh," and she complied.

Tate scanned the living room. The art on the walls, the rugs, and the furniture—everything there looked expensive. None of it looked like anything he'd seen before. The place must've been worth a million bucks.

The ceiling creaked. Someone was walking around upstairs. Tate looked over at the staircase near the kitchen then ascended the stairs as quietly as he could. Sticks didn't follow him. Instead, he began going through drawers.

When Tate got to the top of the stairs, he heard a shower turn on. He glanced into a few of the bedrooms then tiptoed to the bathroom. The door was open a crack. Inside, Sharon was standing in front of the mirror, stripping off her clothes. He stared at her as she slipped off her bra. But as she pulled her spandex down over her thighs, she happened to glance over at the door. Their eyes caught each other's, and there was an instant of silence before she screamed.

Tate went to push into the bathroom, but she slammed the door and locked it. He leaned back and bashed his heel into the door. He did it again and again, sending splinters flying all over the hallway. The door flew open and slammed into the wall before bouncing back. The bathroom was massive, larger than most apartments he'd had. Tate crept inside. He went to the darkened walk-in closet and flipped on the light.

A thick shower rod smashed into his nose. He saw stars and instantly felt tears running from his eyes. The pain radiated into his head. "Fuck!" His hand went to his nose, which was already gushing blood into his mouth and over his chin.

She swung again. He blocked the club with his forearms. Reaching back, he whipped his arm with as much force as he could. The back of his hand impacted against her mouth and sent her flying into a row of men's suits. Tate grabbed her hair and slammed her into the wall before flinging her to the floor. She wasn't moving.

His gushing blood had already stained the carpet in the closet. Tate lifted his soaked ski mask. The liquid dripped down as if his nose were connected to a faucet. Plugging his nose with his fingers, he walked out of the closet and leaned against the sink. He shoved a thick wad of toilet paper up each nostril.

Sticks ran in. He looked from Tate to Sharon, who was nearly unconscious, and then disappeared into the bedroom.

Through the tinted-glass window over the bathtub, Tate stared down at the passing cars, catching his breath. Then he rose and pulled Sharon up. He pulled a pair of handcuffs from his pocket and slapped them on her wrists. She was aware enough that she began struggling, and he smacked the back of her head.

"If you try to run," he said, spitting blood, "I'll kill you."

He dragged her down to the main floor then to the front door. He looked out, making sure no one was around. The RV was only fifty feet away. They could run there in less than fifteen or twenty seconds.

"Hey," Hiapo said. "What about her?" He motioned to the young girl pinned underneath him.

"Bring her with us."

Night in a rich neighborhood didn't feel like nighttime in a poor neighborhood. Tate had lived in places where he didn't feel safe even with his piece. But the street was completely quiet. No one would think about robbing one of the houses with fancy alarms and in a neighborhood with a quick police response. He chuckled to himself.

He dragged the fighting woman out and over the massive lawn. She screamed once. He kicked her in the stomach, and she quieted down. Dragging her was too much effort, so he lifted her by her hair and forced her to walk beside him. If any of the neighbors saw, they might just think she was simply having a casual stroll with Tate.

Carrying the young girl over his shoulder, Hiapo was right behind Tate. Sticks wasn't anywhere to be seen. As Tate reached for the RV door, he stopped. Catching only movement at first, Tate turned his head to see a boy, maybe eleven or twelve, on a bike. His mouth was wide open, and his eyes were locked onto Tate.

"Your mask, bra," Hiapo said.

He had forgotten he'd pulled off his mask in the bathroom. The boy was staring right at Tate's face.

"Let it go," Hiapo said.

Tate opened the RV door and threw Sharon inside. He whipped around and pulled out his pistol from his waistband. His first shot missed, but the second hit the boy in the cheek, flinging him off his bike.

"Your face wasn't the one he saw," Tate said. "Now throw his ass in the bushes, and let's go."

Sticks came running out of the house, his arms full of jewelry. He tripped once on the lawn and fell flat on his face before he rose again and sprinted for the RV. He looked down at the little body on the sidewalk. "Holy shit. What happened?"

"Hurry the fuck up!" Tate shouted.

Sharon was screaming, and he grabbed a roll of duct tape out of his bag of supplies. He taped her mouth then her wrists. Hiapo climbed into the RV after having moved the boy, and he stood glaring down at Tate, the young girl still on his shoulder.

"How 'bout you get goin' so we don't get pinched?"

Hiapo grunted and flung the girl into the passenger seat. Then he got into the driver's side and started the RV. Several neighbors had come out of their homes.

Finished with the tape, Tate dragged Sharon to the back and threw her onto the bed. She kicked at him, making him chuckle. Laughing, he grabbed her tits and made her squeal.

Tate walked to the center of the RV and sat in the built-in table. He glanced out the window at the boy's body. His feet were sticking out of the bushes, and the front tire of the bike still spun gently.

14

The office was nearly empty. It was well past ten o'clock, and most of the attorneys and all the staff had gone home. But Richard Miller sat at his desk, tapping a pen against his shoe. He threw the pen onto the desk and rubbed the bridge of his nose. He'd had a headache all day, and no matter how many Excedrin he took, it wouldn't go away.

Maybe his scheme had been a mistake. Maybe he should call it off. He was bound to get something in the divorce. But if he didn't, he would lose everything else. Richard's father-in-law was a controlling partner at the firm, and he'd given Richard the job. And if he didn't get any money or property, he would be left destitute in the most expensive region of the most expensive state in the nation.

He sighed and rose. He hadn't wanted it to come to this—any of it. All he wanted was a nice marriage to a girl who loved him and plenty of kids. He'd grown up in a family of five and remembered how much fun it was to have four best friends who could never leave him. He wanted that for Eliza. But he wouldn't get it with Sharon. She'd had her tubes tied years before.

Richard stretched his back, and headed out. He waved to one of the custodians, but the man didn't notice him.

The air outside was clean and fresh, though it had a tint of fog to it. A light wetness in the nose. Richard ambled to his car and lay on the hood for a moment, staring at the stars. Hawaii, even Honolulu with all its bright lights, had the best view of the sky he'd ever seen, except for North Dakota. He'd worked there briefly as a floor hand in the oil fields. There, the stars and galaxies above him appeared like a magical painting in the night.

Richard got into his Cadillac and drove home. Because of the light traffic, the drive was quick and pleasant. He checked his watch. It should be done. His heart was pounding, and his guts felt bound up tight.

Without warning, a rush of vomit rose in his throat. He swallowed it but had to pull over to the shoulder of the highway. He stuck his head out the driver's side window, and his lunch came spilling out. When he was through, he sat back in the driver's seat and wiped his lips with the back of his sleeve. Then he headed home.

Everything seemed in order as he rolled to a stop in front of his house. He parked in the driveway because he wanted to make sure all his neighbors saw that he was home. As he walked to his door, he took out his keys and glanced around. Lights were on in other homes, but no one was out. No one was ever out in his neighborhood. Before he turned around, he noticed a child's bike on the sidewalk. No one stole anything there. He had no doubt he could leave money on the sidewalk, and it would still be there the next morning.

As Richard slid the key into the lock, the door opened. He stood frozen, staring at the opening. He pushed it open the rest of the way. The house seemed untouched. He took a step inside. "Hello? Eliza? Sharon?"

He stood in the middle of the large atrium, waiting for a response. But there was complete silence. No televisions. No laptops. No iPads. He shut the door behind him and turned to his empty house.

He did a quick search of the house and found no one in any of the bedrooms, the den, the study, the kitchen, or the pantry. A few things were a little messy—drawers were left open and such—but all in all, the house looked the same as it always did.

He headed upstairs and looked around. Still nothing. Richard took out his cell phone and dialed Eliza's number. The call went to voicemail.

"Hi, Eliza. This is your father. Please call me. I need to know whose house you're staying in at this hour. If you're going to spend the night, please give me or your moth—well, give me a call and let me know. We still have rules here, young lady."

With a sigh, he hung up. Eliza didn't like sleeping at home, and Richard didn't blame her. Once, Eliza had walked in on Sharon's swingers' party. Richard had arrived home to find people having sex on the couch, the kitchen counters, the floors, his antique chairs, the desk in his study, and even on the living room coffee table. As he searched the home for his wife, to have her kick everyone out—they paid no attention when he asked them to leave—Eliza walked in. Her eyes met Richard's, then she walked out. She didn't come home for three days. Richard had to track her down at one of her friend's homes and force her to come back.

Richard's muscles felt tight, and his stomach was a ball of anxiety. He wanted to call Tate, but he knew he should give him some space and let the man work. It would get done. And if it didn't, that wouldn't be the worst thing. In fact, he already regretted acting on the urge. He'd been hurt one too many times, and the impulse just got the better of him.

Maybe he could still call the whole thing off? Just pay Tate ten or twenty thousand to keep quiet and consider the deal a costly mistake? He decided a hot shower would help his thinking process.

Richard walked into his bathroom and began to strip. As he was about to pull his shirt over his head, he saw something on the carpets—dark stains, as if someone had spilled coffee. The splotches and spatters led to a ski mask in the middle of his bathroom floor. Richard's arms dropped, and he leaned against the sink.

They had been here. The blood was… no. How could they be so stupid? The police would clearly find the blood. They couldn't have been that stupid.

Richard searched the closet. Nothing.

A thought hit him, and he froze. He pulled out his cell phone. Tate answered on the first ring.

"Thought you'd be callin'."

"Did you take my daughter?"

"Yeah, she's here."

"What the damn hell is going on? She wasn't a part of this in any way."

"Yeah, well, things change."

"Things change? Things *change*? You kidnap my daughter, and that's all you can say to me?"

"Hey, chill out, man. We haven't done nothin' to her. She's just insurance."

"Insurance for what?"

"To make sure we get paid, man. We get our money as promised. You get your daughter back."

Richard sat down on the edge of the bathtub. "Is it…"

"Nah, man, not yet. But we'll get to it real soon. Probably tonight. We drivin' out right now."

Richard stared at the carpet. He wanted to tell Tate to stop, that it was madness, and they were sure to get caught. But those words didn't come. All that came out was, "There's blood all over my bathroom."

"It's cool, man. Call the cops. Tell them you came home, and that's what you found."

"Are you crazy? The husband's always the prime suspect in these things. At least that's what I see on the news."

"You're a suspect regardless, man. At least this way, you're the one that call them. Ya see?"

"Yeah, yeah, I guess that makes sense. So I just call them and say there's blood everywhere and my wife and daughter are missing?"

"Yeah, man. And you'll get your daughter back. Don't sweat it. Just insurance. I won't touch a hair on her head."

He swallowed. "You should've told me. This wasn't our deal."

"It is what it is. Now we both got work to do. Better get to it."

Richard hung up and placed the phone down on the tub. He rubbed his face and ran his fingers through his hair. He stood up, slammed his fist into the mirror, and screamed. The mirror cracked, and his hand began to bleed.

"Ow. Shit. Shit, shit, shit!"

He picked up his phone again and dialed 9-1-1.

15

Stanton was in a car surrounded by darkness. As the vehicle sped down the road, the lines on the road became a blur. The harder he tried to peer into the darkness, the less he saw. He tried to brake, but nothing happened when his foot pressed the pedal... *Buzz*...

Stanton opened his eyes and recognized the ceiling in his bedroom. The window was open, letting in the ocean breeze, and he could hear the waves crackling outside. His cell phone was vibrating on his nightstand. He answered without checking the ID.

"This is Jon."

"Jon, sorry to wake you. This is Laka."

"Yeah," he said, rubbing the sleep from his eyes.

"We're on call tonight and just caught one up at Diamond Head. A young boy."

"I'll be right down."

Stanton sat up then remained motionless on the bed. He counted five waves outside before getting to his feet and walking over to his balcony. The sky was still as black as tar during that odd moment in which night had passed, but morning hadn't come. The ocean reflected the moonlight as a wet, wavy glow.

He dressed in a blazer and jeans then grabbed his .45 Desert Eagle and its holster. The gun was never far away from him. He used to be able to leave it in the kitchen or living room, but not anymore. He'd taken to keeping it in his bedroom, no more than a few feet away from him when he slept. He felt different at night after a decade of being a cop.

He turned on the alarm as he left the house. He started his Jeep, pulled out of his driveway, and headed toward H1.

Stanton was familiar with Diamond Head. Most people associated it with the beach and surfing. But it was also one of the most expensive neighborhoods in Honolulu. Some of the beachfront properties there could run up to twenty million. He'd been there once with his fiancée, Emma. She had a friend there whose husband had made his money in derivatives.

The highway was clear. Only the occasional car passed him. The wind whipped through his hair and over his face. It screamed in his ears, and he stuck his arm over the side of the Jeep and let it dangle.

The exit was surrounded by lush trees and yellow-and-red plants. The streets were well kept, and none of the buildings suffered from the usual wear and tear of Hawaii's rain damage, which made all the buildings appear twenty years older than they were. Everything was new there.

Stanton found the address and spotted the police cruisers parked out front. The medical examiner's van was already there. So was the Scientific Investigation Section's SUV.

Stanton sat in his Jeep for a moment. Every time he drove to the scene of a homicide, he had to prepare himself. No homicide was clean or neat. Nothing like on television or in Agatha Christie books. Homicides were always gory. Blood work.

He stepped out of the Jeep and causally strolled to where Laka was standing with a uniformed officer. Neighbors were watching through windows.

In the bushes nearby, the legs of a child were sticking out.

"Hey," she said when she saw him.

Stanton stood next to her. "Hey. What do we have?"

"The homeowner, Richard Miller, called in a kidnapping. Said his wife and daughter were missing. The responding officers took a look around the lawn and saw this poor kid."

"Do we know who he is yet?"

She shook her head. "No ID, obviously. We'll just have to canvas the neighborhood. Unless he was shot somewhere else and then dumped here."

Stanton kneeled over the boy's body. He had a gunshot wound in his cheek. The round had torn through the bone and exploded the back of his head. There couldn't be much brain matter left in the skull, since most of it was on the sidewalk.

"No," he said, "he was shot here." Stanton looked up at the trees and down both sides of the street. "One shot, up close. Definitely not a drive-by shooting. Someone specifically wanted him dead."

"Why would you want a kid dead?"

Stanton stood and closed his eyes. He said a quick, silent prayer for the boy and his family before turning away. "If you thought you had something to gain."

"Like what?"

"I don't know. Is Richard Miller inside?"

"Yeah. He was hysterical when he found out someone had been killed."

Stanton headed toward the house. The home was massive—it had at least eight or nine bedrooms. Stanton stopped to peer through the passenger window of the brand new Cadillac in the driveway. The inside was spotless. Stanton turned back toward the house and ambled through the front door. He stopped in the atrium and scanned the house. The spacious layout was meant to keep people away from each other if they wanted. A family could live in the house for decades and not have to see each other.

Two officers and a man on the couch waited in the living room. The man's shoulders were slumped, and he was sipping from a mug. The two officers were chatting. From the top of the staircase and to the right, other voices floated down—probably the forensic techs. He decided to head up there first.

The second floor was as spacious as the first. Stanton didn't get lost only because he could hear the voices coming from the master bedroom. He counted eight rooms as he passed them. The master was probably the biggest and most elegantly decorated of them all. He had to stop a moment and just take it in. The bed was the largest he'd ever seen, almost like three king-sized beds pushed together. French doors opened onto a large balcony, where a small fountain with koi fish was tucked away. Stanton strolled out and stood over the fish as they glided through the clear water.

"Detective," a woman behind him said. Debbie Cunningham from the SIS section was dressed in black with an SIS badge over her chest and latex gloves covering her hands. Stanton noticed her wearing a necklace he'd never seen before. A Tibetan symbol of peace.

"How are you, Debbie?"

"Fine, other than I'm hating having to go out and look at a young kid this early in the morning."

"Every vic has a story to tell. Without it, we can't catch who did this."

"I didn't say I wasn't gonna do it. I just hate having to."

Stanton glanced once more at the koi then stepped inside the bedroom. "What did you find?"

"Blood all over the carpets and a ski mask soaked from the inside. Looks like someone got a piece of him. Maybe broke his nose. The blood on the carpet was tail-end pointing inward, which means he got hit in the closet and then backed out."

"Someone was hiding in there and hurt him," Stanton said.

"That'd be my guess."

"Anything else?"

"Not really. Some shoeprints in the atrium. I have Billy out with the vic. We'll see if anything turns up there."

"Keep me posted," Stanton said, gently brushing past her to look into the walk-in closet.

"I will." She hesitated. "And Jon?"

"Yeah?"

"We went out bowling last night. You didn't come."

"No, not really my thing."

"We're gonna head out for drinks with some of the boys from Vice tonight. That's always a party. You wanna come?"

He grinned. "I don't drink."

"Oh, I didn't mean… I mean, I meant it, but I thought—"

"I'd love to come," he said.

She smiled, and he turned back to the closet.

16

Tate glanced back once at the young girl. She was sitting in the back of the RV on the bed, with her arms folded and a scowl on her face. Sticks was sitting across from her in a chair, smoking a joint. He was eyeing her as though he were about to do something. Tate would have to watch him. Nobody got first before him.

"She's mine," Tate yelled.

"What?" Sticks asked. Hiapo, who'd been sleeping on the floor, also looked up.

"They're both mine. Nobody's doin' shit to 'em until I say so. I'm not getting sloppy seconds from you two gonorrhea-havin' muthafuckers."

Sticks mumbled some profanity and turned his eyes back toward the girl. Tate could hear him speaking to her.

"What's your name?" Sticks asked.

"Eliza."

"What are you, like in eighth grade?"

"Ninth."

"Oh yeah? That's when I dropped out. Ninth grade. You play sports?"

The girl didn't answer right away. "Soccer."

"You like playin' with balls, huh? I got some balls you can play with."

Sticks let out a high-pitched laugh. Tate watched him in the rearview and shook his head.

He'd thrown Sharon into the bathroom. She'd screamed and thumped against the walls for a few minutes, but she'd been quiet ever since Hiapo had gone in there.

Tate looked at the clock on the dash. It was almost daybreak. They were supposed to meet Lee around noon, but he decided he was going to wake him up instead. Lee lived in a section of Oahu known as Princeville. Tate parked in front of Lee's rundown house, which was away from the beach. He glanced around to see if anyone was out, but it was too early in the morning for people to be outside.

"Wait here," Tate said.

He stepped out and looked both ways before sauntering up to the front door of the home and knocking. He knocked again then pounded with his fist. A light came on. Lee answered, looking groggy and wearing boxer shorts.

"Tate? What the fuck you doin' here?"

"I wanna get these bitches outta here, yo."

"Now? It's like four in the mornin', man. Ain't no one buyin' bitches at four in the mornin'."

"It's cool. I'll wait."

Tate pushed his way into the home and flopped onto the couch. A bong was on the coffee table next to a baggie of weed. He packed some weed into the bong and took the lighter out of his pocket. Lee sat in the beat-up recliner across from him and rubbed his eyes.

After taking a long toke, Tate let it out slowly through his nose. "How much you think we'd get?"

"I dunno," Lee said, rocking back and forth slowly. "You ever been in the pimp game?"

"Nah, man. I mean, a little. I had this girl up in this apartment complex. She thought she loved me, and I'd get her out to the other dudes in the complex. Rent her out for a night an' shit. But I ain't been serious in the game." He took another long pull. The weed was weak, but it'd been sprinkled with something. Coke or X.

"I been in the game since back in the day. Back when I was a young buck, man, had me three girls. I'd sit on my ass in a hotel room and take 'em from city to city, ya know."

"How much you make in a day?"

"Depend on the city, man. But if the girl's fine, she get more. I had this one bitch that was like a model, ya know? She made me like two G's a day."

"Shit."

"I know."

Tate took another long pull then said, "I'm really fuckin' high."

"Take it easy on that shit, yo."

"What's in—"

A scream came from outside, loud enough that Tate and Lee both stared at each other.

"Shit!"

Tate jumped up and sprinted outside. He ran to the RV, opened the door, and flew inside. Sticks was on top of the girl, trying to get her shorts off. Tate ran up and wrapped his arm around Sticks's throat. He lifted the man, who was foaming at the mouth, off the girl and threw him to the floor. Tate kicked him in the ribs as hard as he could then spun Sticks onto his back.

"What'd I say?" Tate shouted. "What'd I say, huh? Don't touch 'em 'til I say so." He looked at Hiapo, who was laying on the floor, looking up at them. "And where were you?"

Hiapo closed his eyes again. "Ain't my problem."

Tate stepped over to the girl. She was shaking and crying. Tate stared at her but didn't say anything. She quieted but continued trembling, and he turned and left the RV. Lee was standing outside.

"Man, don't be bringin' your rapist-ass muthafuckers up in my place."

Tate took out his 9mm and placed it against Lee's forehead. The two men's eyes locked. Tate saw fear in Lee's eyes. He didn't know what Lee saw in his eyes.

"Hey, man, I'm just sayin'. I got neighbors."

Tate tucked the gun back in his waistband. "Get your boy over here, and we'll bounce."

"A'ight, man. I'll call him. Just chill, a'ight. We cool."

Tate watched him walk into the house. He turned back to the RV, where Sticks sat at the table, scowling at him. Tate pulled out a cigarette and lit it, then leaned against the RV, smoking as he stared into the dark sky.

17

Stanton examined every inch of the Millers' home. From the massive pool and hot tub out back to the pantry containing only gourmet supplies. He was informed by one of the responding officers that the Millers had a chef who came five nights a week, but they hadn't been able to reach him. Stanton opened a file on the Millers in his phone and made a note to follow up with the chef.

The boy outside had been identified: Adam Gilmore Cummings, eleven years old. His family lived four houses to the south, and they had reported the boy missing a couple of hours before. Stanton was glad he didn't have to be the one to notify them that their son had been found.

Stanton was outside as the medical examiner's people zipped up the body and hauled it away. The techs had found gunshot residue on the boy's forehead, indicating he'd been shot from no more than five feet away. If the shooter had been any farther away than that, only a few particles from the explosive primer or propellant would have been present, probably not enough to detect.

Stanton had saved Richard Miller's interview for last. He had called in only the kidnappings, and he was adamant that he hadn't known about the murder.

Richard was sitting on a fine white couch when Stanton approached him. Amber liquid and ice filled the tumbler in front of him. Stanton could smell the alcohol on his breath from practically ten feet away.

"Richard, my name is Detective Jon Stanton. I'm with the Homicide Detail of the Honolulu Police Department. I'm one of the detectives investigating this case."

Richard nodded but didn't say anything. His eyes drifted over the room, as though he were taking it in for the first time. Stanton sat next to him, as close as he could without touching him. Richard was displaying signs of nervousness and agitation. Stanton thought he might be able to push him a little further with a slight discomfort.

"Your wife's name is Sharon, and your daughter is Eliza. Thirteen, is that right?"

"Yes."

"And the last time you saw either your wife or your daughter was this morning when you left for work?"

"Yes, that's correct. I leave at eight every morning. When I got home in the evening, this is what I found."

"My partner said you were surprised when she informed you of the young boy's body outside."

"What kind of question is that? Of course I was surprised. You wouldn't be surprised if your neighbor's corpse was found outside your house?"

Stanton placed his elbows on his knees, leaning slightly forward to give the impression of relaxation. "You didn't see him when you pulled in?"

Richard shook his head and looked down to the carpet. "No, I saw his bike. But I thought one of the neighborhood kids had just left it out. This is a really safe neighborhood, and people leave things out."

Stanton remained silent for a moment. Most people didn't handle silence well. They would rather say something—anything—to avoid sitting in silence with a stranger. Richard's reaction was even more overblown than the average reaction Stanton had seen. He began rubbing his hands together, and his eyes darted around the room, occasionally landing on Stanton's face.

"Is there anyone that would want to hurt you or your family?"

"No. Not that I can think of."

"I was told you're an attorney. Any disgruntled clients?"

He scoffed. "They're all disgruntled, Detective. Take your pick."

"Does your wife have any enemies that you know of?"

He shook his head. "No. I don't have a clue who would want to hurt my wife and daughter. We keep to ourselves."

Stanton was an expert in the Facial Action Coding System first published in the late '70s. People unconsciously make small facial movements, called microexpressions, that last only split seconds when relaying information. Generally, people couldn't control their microexpressions. Though the expressions couldn't prove a person was lying, they could prove underlying emotions were not being addressed.

Dr. Paul Ekman pioneered the use of microexpressions to detect deceit, and he co-authored a study known as the *Wizards Project* in the psychological journals. Ekman wanted to know how many people could intuitively read microexpressions well enough to distinguish deception. He called this type of person a "Truth Wizard." Of the twenty thousand participants, only fifty could accurately read microexpressions well enough to tell if another person was being deceptive.

Stanton, a graduate student in psychology at the time, had been one of the fifty. But Stanton didn't need any of his training or research to know that Richard Miller was being less than truthful. Perhaps he wasn't out-and-out lying, but he wasn't telling the whole story, either. And Richard knew that Stanton knew, and it was making Richard even more uncomfortable.

"Mr. Miller, my only concern is finding who killed that boy, and finding your wife and child. If you know something, you should tell me now."

He glanced at him. "No, I don't know anything. If I did, I would, of course, tell you."

Stanton nodded. "Just so you're aware, the type of man that could kill a young boy from no more than five feet away could do all sorts of horrible things that you might not be able to imagine."

"It's just a terrible, terrible situation. If I hear from them, you will be the first one I call."

Stanton rose. He took a card out of his wallet and left it on the coffee table. "That has my cell. Call anytime, day or night."

"I will."

Stanton scanned the room quickly before he said, "Nice house," and walked away.

18

Stanton met Laka outside, where she was coordinating with the uniforms to interview all the neighbors. He watched her directing the officers. Not a hint of bashfulness or politeness. Just direct authority and power. Her uncle had the same quality.

Stanton hung back until she was done. She turned and caught his eyes, and they both grinned.

"Sorry, I know you're the senior detective here," she said.

"Nothing to be sorry about. You have a presence that they respect."

"Well, presence or a three hundred-pound uncle who's their boss. Either one works for me."

Stanton took in a deep breath and scanned the neighborhood. The sun was coming up, and the sky had turned a dull gray. "We're short uniforms. I'll help canvas the neighbors. Can you make sure to get a written statement from Richard Miller?"

"Sure."

The other officers hadn't yet started canvassing the north side of the street, so Stanton marched in that direction. Canvassing a neighborhood was an odd experience. Officers got an irregular assortment of people from those who welcomed the opportunity to help the police, to those who just wanted them to go away as quickly as possible.

The first house belonged to a middle-aged woman who treated Stanton almost like a door-to-door salesman. She hadn't seen or heard anything. Next was a family, and the father grew upset that the police had dared to come knocking on his door at such a late hour. A single man was next, a business owner who sold shipping containers to large companies and managed to work that into the first few minutes of speaking to Stanton.

"Did you see anything out of the ordinary at all?" Stanton asked him.

"I didn't see anything, but I heard what I guess was a gunshot."

"What time?"

"I don't know, like two. I didn't look at my clock. But I heard this like, *pop*, and it woke me up. I didn't think anything of it."

"Did you hear anything after the pop, like a car driving away?"

"Yeah, yeah, I did actually. A car turned on and took off. But it didn't sound like a car. It was more like a big truck. One of those really big trucks, 'cause the engine was all deep."

"I appreciate your help. If you think of anything else, please let me know." Stanton handed him a card. "Do you know anything about your neighbor, Richard Miller?"

"Rich? No, not really. Other than his wife, I never talked to them."

"What was his wife like?"

The man hesitated.

"It's really important. I'm investigating the death of a young boy, and it just happens that Sharon Miller is missing on the same night."

"She was… flirty."

"Flirty?"

"Yeah, like, she was always hitting on everyone. I know she had an affair with Mark just up the street. It actually broke up his marriage."

"Where does Mark live?"

"That house right there, with the pillars on the front porch."

Stanton looked at the house. It was massive, with a front lawn like a soccer field. "I appreciate your help."

Mark's home was a mansion. Six Corinthian pillars took up the porch. And the property was fenced off. Stanton hopped over the fence. He hoped Mark didn't have a lot of dogs.

A minute after the first doorbell ring, Mark answered the door, wearing only thin, tight underwear that showed off the musculature of his legs. He was a muscular man—overly so, Stanton thought. His arms were the size of melons, and the muscles in his stomach bulged, but the stomach itself was distended, as if he'd just eaten a large meal. He was breathing hard, and sweat was pouring out of him.

"Who the fuck are—"

"I'm Detective Jon Stanton with the Honolulu Police Department. I'm investigating the homicide of one of your neighbors. I had to hop the fence, hope you don't mind."

Anger was drawn on the man's face. "Hell yes, I mind. Why do you think I put the damn fence up?"

Stanton grinned. "I don't know. But I can see the needle marks going up your thigh to your buttocks. If we search this house, how much steroids are we gonna find?"

"You can't search shit. You don't have probable cause."

"The track marks give me probable cause. And coming to speak to you about a murder is a legitimate reason to be at your door. Now, would you like to talk about the murder or about what's in your house?"

The man's face flushed red. His upper lip curled into his mouth as though his anger were so intense that his body just couldn't contain it anymore. Stanton didn't move or flinch. The man's face finally softened. The thought of jail, particularly jail without his steroids where his muscles would wither away, didn't seem to appeal to him.

"What do you want?"

"You had an affair with Sharon Miller, and she's missing now. Where were you last night?"

He sneered. "You think I'd kidnap that ho? She'd fuck anything that moves anytime. No one would need to kidnap her."

"She was promiscuous?"

"No, she wasn't promiscuous. I had a girlfriend in high school that was promiscuous. Sharon was a nymphomaniac. She went to this theater once and did an orgy with like five dudes. Didn't know any of them, just went to a movie theater and got guys to go into the back of the theater and do it. I found out that kinda shit later. After we were done. And I was right here asleep in my bed all night. My car hasn't moved."

"She told your wife about you two?"

"Yeah. She actually asked my wife if she was interested in a three-way. That's how my wife found out. Sharon was so fucking stupid, she didn't realize that normal people don't do stuff like that when they're married."

"Did she and Richard belong to any swingers' clubs that you know of?"

"Richard didn't. Sharon used to tease him that he couldn't get another woman. I always felt bad for the little dude."

"But not bad enough to stop sleeping with his wife."

"Hey, that's life. The strongest get the women."

Stanton glanced into Mark's home. Weights were spread out over the living room, and posters of half-naked girls covered the walls. "And who gets your woman now?"

It was a low blow, but Mark deserved it. His anger had returned, and a vein in his neck was sticking out. But Stanton already had what he needed from him. He would put Mark on a list of suspects for the SIS unit to test for gunshot residue.

"Thanks for your time," Stanton said as he stepped off the porch.

"Hey, how'd you see the track marks?"

"I didn't," Stanton said with a smile. He hopped over the fence again and landed on his heels on the other side.

The day dragged on slowly. There were at least sixty homes Stanton wanted checked, and he had only two officers to help him do it. By noon, sweat stuck to his back and dripped down his forehead into his eyes.

Stanton sat down on the curb, the hot island sun on the back of his neck, and took off his shoes. He stripped off his soaked socks then put his shoes back on. The officers were making their way toward the three remaining houses. It was time to head into the precinct, and he had almost nothing to show for his efforts.

After several hours of walking, the drive in the Jeep felt like heaven. Stanton stopped at a drive-thru and ordered a turkey sandwich with mango jelly, chips, and a Diet Coke. He ate on the road as he drove back into downtown.

Once back at the precinct, he dabbed at a spot of food on his shirt before heading up to the bullpen and his desk. The homicide table— his portion of the division—was nearly empty. Everyone was out for lunch or working cases. He sat quietly at his desk and transcribed the notes in his phone into a Word document on his computer. He checked the Spillman database and ran a few of Richard Miller's neighbors' names through, hoping he'd come back with a few priors for kidnapping or sex offenses, but the worst that came back was a white-collar fraud case and a few DUIs.

Stanton noticed Kai in his office. The big man was eating a sandwich half as long as his desk, and when he saw Stanton, he nodded. Stanton walked over and sat across from him.

"You want some?" Kai asked.

"I ate. Thanks. Can I ask you something, though?"

"Sure."

"Are you trying to set me up with your niece?"

Kai grinned and took a bite of the sandwich. "Why not?"

"You've seen my luck with relationships, Kai. I'm not the ideal husband over here."

"You got a good job, you don't drink or smoke, you go to church every Sunday, and you'd never raise a hand to her. What more can an uncle ask for?"

"She needs someone younger. I'm not sure I could keep up."

"You haven't even been on one date. Take her out and see how you feel."

"Maybe." Stanton tapped his fingers against the desk. "She's gonna make a great detective. You should see her with the uniforms. Totally calm and in charge. No second-guessing."

"She's always been like that. She played football in middle school just because they said girls couldn't play. She was good, too. Receiver. She could run faster than any of them boys." He wiped his lips with a napkin then took a long drink out of his jug of soda. "I saw the kid up on the board. Eleven years old, huh?"

"Yeah. Parents still together. They had to be informed this morning that their son died."

Kai shook his head. "That is the one thing I ain't never liked about this job. Never. Some people can make the families feel better. I can't. It was always hard."

"Me, too. Anything I say just comes off as empty."

He leaned back in his seat, loosening his belt a little. "What you think of the boy?"

"I don't think it's random."

"It might just be a drive-by shooting. Maybe teenagers trying to shoot the house and hitting the boy."

"No, I don't think so. It was close range. And the neighborhood's upscale, not the type of place for a drive-by shooting. The blood spatter and tissues were on the sidewalk, too. He wasn't found on the sidewalk. He was found in the bushes. Someone moved his body. A drive-by shooter wouldn't do that. They would shoot and then get the heck out of there as quickly as they could."

"Somebody he knew?"

"I don't think so. I think he came upon something he shouldn't have. It might not have even been last night. He could've seen something the day before that… a month before, who knows? But I think he saw something he wasn't meant to see. And they did that to him for it. Maybe he saw the kidnappers of Sharon and Eliza Miller."

Kai shook his head and leaned forward for another bite of the sandwich. "Well, if anyone can find the *laho kole*, it's you. But you got enough on your plate. Technically, child crimes goes to JSD. Give the case over to them if you want."

Stanton was quiet for a moment. He certainly had other cases to work. The board—the homicide whiteboard up near the bullpen—had eighteen open and active homicides, six of which were his. In the Honolulu PD, as in most major police departments, anything having to do with children—from child abuse and sex crimes, to child murder—was handled by a special child crimes section. In San Diego, when Stanton had been there, it was called the Child Abuse Unit. In Honolulu, it was the Juvenile Services Division. Though they had a broader mission here in terms of education and following up on runaways, child crimes were their specialty. Their detectives received specialized training to deal with parents and relatives as well as suspects and victims. Perhaps they would be better suited to handle the case than Stanton would have been.

"So," Kai said, "what's it gonna be? You want it or not?"

Stanton thought back to the boy's body. He'd been thrown into the bushes like a sack of refuse. No dignity had been shown to him whatsoever. "No, I'll take it."

Kai shrugged. "It's yours. Go get the *ule malules*."

19

The morning light bothered him. Richard rolled one way on the bed then the other. But no matter where he was, he couldn't get comfortable. The alarm clock went off, and he slammed it with his fist, but it kept beeping. So he unplugged it and pushed it off the nightstand.

Inhaling deeply, he fixed his eyes on the ceiling. He couldn't help but think that things had gone from bad to worse. The police were involved, and that creepy detective had sat right next to him and stared at his face without even blinking. Richard hadn't known a single person could unnerve him like that. Even Sharon's father, the most intimidating man Richard had ever met, could be dealt with in his own way. But that detective's gaze had bored into Richard's head, and he'd lost his cool. Clearly, the detective knew he was hiding something.

Richard finally rose to get ready for the day. He liked to have music on when he dressed. That was, at least when Sharon wasn't home to yell at him about it. He turned on Mozart's *Serenade* and took his time browsing the plethora of suits hanging in his closet.

He finally settled on the gray pinstripe, along with a white-and-black tie, a white-and-black shirt, and a white pocket square. Because his work was almost all transactional, he could wear whatever he wanted to the office, but he always preferred to wear a suit—like the partners did.

The sting his last conversation had about making partner came back to him, and he had to forcibly push it out of his mind. On top of everything else, he'd just realized he was in a dead-end job.

He sat at the table by himself, eating fruit and drinking sparkling water. He thought of Eliza. She was out there with those men, whom he knew nothing about, except that they would do anything for money. But she would be fine. They wouldn't hurt her. They had to know they wouldn't see a dime if they laid a finger on her. And once everything was said and done, he and Eliza would have all the money they could want to do whatever in the world they felt like doing.

After breakfast, Richard cleaned the dish and glass then went outside. The police were gone. He walked to the sidewalk where the Cummings boy's blood was still spattered on the pavement. His bike was gone.

Such a shame. He'd been a friendly boy. Several times, he'd stopped for Richard as he was backing the Cadillac out of the driveway rather than racing past him as most boys would. But that was life, Richard guessed. No one ever achieved anything without somebody getting hurt.

The drive into the office was pleasant, despite the knot in his gut. He grabbed a latté on the way into work then strolled into the office as if nothing were wrong. No one said anything to him, and he, at least that day, preferred it that way.

He shut the door and sat at his desk. He should have been able to do a little work, but it wasn't possible. The thought of planning an estate or writing a will sickened him. He had a client coming in to learn about the tax benefits of different types of corporations, but one of the other associates could easily handle that.

Finally, after an hour of agonizing over it, he took out his cell phone and dialed Tate's number.

"It's done," Tate offered as a greeting.

Richard's heart dropped. "It's… what do you mean by 'it's'?"

"You know what I mean."

He swallowed. "How?"

"One to the head. It's done."

"I want proof."

"What?"

"I want proof."

"We never talked about any proof. You're gonna have to take my word for it."

"Like hell. You want that money? I want proof that she's gone, and I want my daughter back."

Tate was silent for almost too long. "All right. I'll send you a photo."

The line went dead.

Anxiety gnawed at Richard so fiercely that he couldn't sit still. He was pacing his office when Candice walked in.

"Richard, I'm glad you're here. I didn't like our last interaction."

"I really can't talk right now, Candice. I've got some really pressing issues. Really pressing. They just can't wait for anything."

"Well we're all busy, but I'd like to take a moment and discuss a possible partnership track."

His stomach dropped. "What?"

"You've worked hard here, and being Eli's son-in-law certainly doesn't hurt. I think maybe I jumped to conclusions too quickly. How about we bring it up at the next partners' meeting and see what everybody thinks?"

"Okay… yeah, sure. That'd be great."

She smiled and left the room. Richard returned to pacing the office. What the hell was he doing? He'd gotten himself involved in a world he didn't understand, and he had no idea what the rules were. How did the Neanderthals Heather defended commit crimes without an ounce of anxiety or guilt? And why the hell had Candice picked that moment to spring the best news he'd heard in years?

His cell phone rang. He didn't recognize the number.

"This is Richard."

"Mr. Miller, this is Detective Jon Stanton. How are you holding up?"

He hesitated. "I'm fine, Detective. But really busy. If I could call you back, that would really help me."

"Well, I just wanted to have another look through your home. By myself. I was hoping you wouldn't mind."

Richard bit his thumbnail. What the hell else could he want to see? The police had already spent an entire day there. "Um, no. That should be fine. I get off work around eight."

"Well, I'd like to do it sooner if possible. I could send an officer to pick up the key."

"There's no key. It's a code entry." Richard gave him the code.

"I appreciate that."

"So, um, what exactly are you looking for? It seemed like you guys already tore that place apart."

"Things always get overlooked. In the hustle and bustle, you miss things. That's why I like to go back by myself the day after, just make sure everything's how it should be." The conversation took a slight pause, then Stanton said, "So you're back to work already, huh?"

*Shit,* Richard thought. He hadn't considered how that would look. His wife and daughter were missing, and he was back at the office instead of waiting by the phone at home. He couldn't keep track of all the things he was supposed to consider.

"Yeah, just a few things. I… well, between me and you, I can't concentrate enough to work. I thought it would take my mind off this whole thing, but it's just made it worse. I won't be here long."

"Hm. Well, I appreciate the code. I'll make sure to forget it after today."

"No worries. I was thinking of changing it anyway."

After Stanton hung up, Richard tossed his phone across the room. It dented the wall then clattered to the floor.

"Shit!" he said, swinging his arms as if he were hitting something. He marched around his desk a few times then grabbed his keys and ran out of the office.

20

The RV stank of weed and sweat. Eliza Miller was curled in a ball on the bed. The big one called Hiapo was eating at the table in the center. Sticks, the one who had gotten on top of her and tried to rip off her shorts, was passed out. She didn't recognize the smell of what he had been smoking out of his pipe, but it wasn't weed. It smelled like burnt garbage, and he got jittery then smoked weed and drank after using the pipe.

The sun was up, and she felt better in the daylight. Her mother was locked in the bathroom and hadn't come out. Hiapo was far enough away that he might not be able to hear her call out to her mother. And he was busy eating and staring out the window. The third one, Tate, had gone inside the house and hadn't come out since the skinny one had tried to mount her.

"Mom?" she whispered. "Mom, can you hear me?"

After a long silence, a faint voice answered, "Yes. Do you know where we are?"

"No. In some neighborhood."

"Have they said what they wanted?"

"No." She looked at Hiapo. "There's three of them. One's in the house, and the other two are here."

"Where's your phone?"

"They took it. Are you okay?"

"I'm fine, sweetie. When I heard you screaming… I didn't know what to do. I was going crazy."

"I'm scared, Mommy."

"I know. Just stay calm and see if you can find your phone. They have to have it in here somewhere."

Eliza scanned the RV's filthy interior. Empty cereal boxes, pizza containers, and beer cans littered the floor. Her eyes drifted over to Sticks. He was on a couch, twitching in his sleep. The tip of her phone peeked out from the breast pocket of his jacket.

"I see my phone," she whispered.

"Can you reach it?"

"I don't know."

Sticks was out and hadn't been up for at least half an hour. Hiapo was sitting with his back to Sticks. She thought she could sneak up there without the big one noticing. She swallowed, slipped off her shoes, and stepped onto the carpet.

The carpet made her feet itch, and her heart was pounding so hard that she was scared they could hear it. She closed her eyes. Just a few days ago, a boy had asked her to the school dance. Thomas Ovard. She'd been hoping he would ask. He played football and was muscular yet lean. She'd liked him from the moment she'd met him in an English class. He wasn't smart and didn't seem to care about school, so he always copied off her. But she didn't mind. She enjoyed helping him.

Since he'd asked, she'd thought of nothing but the dance—until she'd found herself stuck in an RV with a group of men. Tate had crazy eyes that told her he was on the edge of losing his mind. He was the most frightening man she'd ever met. But he was the only thing keeping Sticks from raping her.

As slowly as she could, she tiptoed down the length of the RV. Hiapo was busy with his food. He was watching something on his phone and would chuckle to himself every few seconds then look out the window. She could see out the windows, too. If she could make it outside, she could scream her head off, and someone might come out to help. But it might not matter. Tate might just shoot them the way he'd shot her neighbor, Adam.

The couch wasn't far, and Sticks was snoring. Eliza stood over him. She had to force her trembling hands to stop moving. Her hand, almost on its own, reached out for the phone. She could feel it. All she needed to do was get it and text her dad. He would do everything else.

Eliza placed her thumb and finger on the sides. She glanced over at the big one, but he wasn't paying attention to anything but the video on his phone. She lifted, slipping it lightly out of the pocket about halfway. Holding her breath, she pulled up and got the phone all the way out.

It was almost in her pocket when Sticks grabbed her wrist. She gasped, and their eyes locked. A wicked grin crossed his face.

"Little bitch!"

He reached up and smacked her. She jerked away and screamed, running to the back of the RV. She opened the bathroom door, instinctively hoping her mother could protect her. But when she saw her mother, fear and despair filled her. Her mother was bound with duct tape and was sitting on the toilet. She had urinated on herself, her right eye was swollen shut, and her lips were cut and coated in dried blood.

Sticks seized Eliza by the hair and threw her onto the bed. He took off his belt and folded it in half. As he raised it to whip her, a meaty brown hand grasped his arm and ripped away the belt.

"Tate said not to touch her," Hiapo bellowed.

"Fuck him. And fuck you, too."

"Sit down."

Sticks got in the big man's face. "I said—fuck. You."

Hiapo started to turn away then suddenly spun back. He wrapped his fingers around Sticks's throat and lifted him into the air as if he were a doll. He flung him against the wall, shaking the entire RV.

Sticks reached into his waistband to the pistol tucked away there. Hiapo took one of Sticks's fingers and bent it all the way back until—*snap!* Sticks screamed, and Hiapo snatched the gun and put it into his own waistband.

"You broke my fucking finger!"

"Tate said not to touch her."

Sticks got to his feet, cradling his hand. The finger was bent at an angle that made it appear useless. He stormed out of the RV and slammed the door behind him. Hiapo looked the women over. He grunted something then went back to his video.

21

The ocean was far warmer than it appeared. The sun was just barely breaking through the clouds, and its beams danced around it like ashes dancing around the glowing embers of a fire. Stanton paddled far out from shore and drifted lightly on the waves before turning back. He'd caught his set almost half an hour ago and was through, but didn't want to leave the sea just yet.

Some people did their best thinking in their sleep, on the toilet, or in the quiet shade of a tree. Stanton did his on the ocean. He lost himself there amid something greater than himself. The ocean would exist long after man's turn at ruling the earth was over. But being the ruler was man's illusion. The ocean ruled the earth. However the oceans went, the earth would go, as well.

Stanton rode a weak wave in to the shore then stood in the hip-deep water. He straightened his board and trudged onto the beach. A small crowd of younger surfers was out there with him, and they were already drunk or splitting bowls of weed. They were missing the point. They couldn't appreciate the grandeur if their senses were dulled.

Stanton showered on the beach and changed into jeans and a red polo shirt. He had left a message for his kids to call him, but they hadn't yet. Teenagers had their own lives to live.

As he climbed into the Jeep, Stanton thought about Richard Miller. The day before, he had called and asked to see Richard's house, just to see what Richard would say. He'd seemed apprehensive about it. Stanton let it go and decided to stop by the house a day later.

He drove down there before going to morning roll call at the precinct. The reports from the previous night and updates to the detective commander and the captain could wait.

Stanton pulled to a stop in front of the home. He never would have even guessed that a murder had taken place there not two days before. Some murder and suicide scenes healed immediately, without leaving behind evidence of the foul occurrence. But a handful retained… something. Stanton had heard it called energy, essence, ghosts, phantoms, demons, spirits, and everything in between.

He had once seen a home where the oldest son, a paranoid schizophrenic, had murdered his entire family. Parents and three siblings. Six years later, in the same home, a husband murdered his wife. The couple had bought the home from a shady realtor who hadn't revealed its past. Stanton didn't believe in coincidences.

Stanton got out and ambled across the street to the sidewalk in front of the home, where Adam Cummings had been killed. He closed his eyes.

*I see your face. You're looking at me, and I know what you see. You see me, and I see you. And we both know we shouldn't be here. I can't let you live. I take out my gun and fire. I'm so close to you that I can't miss. You fly off your feet and hit the pavement. I need to leave—a gunshot just went off in a quiet neighborhood, but I'm calm. I'm not rushed or panicked. I move or have the body moved into the bushes. I don't care that you're young. I don't care that you're just a boy. You're nothing to me...*

Stanton opened his eyes and turned to the bushes where the body had been found. He stared at it a long time then sauntered across the lawn to the front porch of the Millers' home. A fine microfiber couch and two matching chairs sat on the large porch. A side table had a book on it. *The Kite Runner.* Stanton opened it to the bookmark, which was about halfway through the book, and read parts of the page. He wondered if the book belonged to Richard or his wife. He set it back on the side table and entered the code on the door.

He didn't know if Richard was still home. The man would be jumpy and probably armed. Stanton would have to be careful.

The atrium looked as though it belonged in a fancy office building rather than a private residence. Everything in the home matched the island theme. A designer had carefully selected everything to give one the impression that visitors were entering an oasis and leaving the humdrum of normal life. It was a very pleasant place to come home to. But Stanton didn't think it was for the Millers.

The home looked even more massive in the daylight than it had before. It was far too much house for a couple and one teenager. Either they were just trying to impress the outside world, or they had bought it with an expectation of many more children.

Though infidelity had many causes, Stanton guessed he knew what had caused Sharon Miller to seek sex outside of her marriage. Despite the stereotype of the cheating, horny male, clinical research had proven without a doubt that women cheated as often as men did—in some contexts, even more. Stanton thought this was so hard for most people to accept simply because of the fragile male ego.

The motivations, however, did fall into the conventional gender roles. The most extensive study ever done on infidelity examined a dating website that catered to married men and women looking for extramarital affairs. Roughly sixty percent of the women in the study said they felt emotional love for the objects of their affair, whereas only seven percent of men said they felt love for the objects of their affair. For men, it was purely physical, but women sought the emotional connection.

The primary reason the women reported for beginning the affair was feeling neglected or ignored by their husbands. This led to a lack of intimacy. Women who were also lonely tended to lean toward affairs if their husbands were gone for long periods of time or frequently away overnight for work.

Stanton guessed Sharon Miller's affairs had nothing to do with feeling neglected. Richard struck him as passive. He would do anything to keep his wife happy.

Intimacy disorders were often diagnosed in adulterous women. Typically, they stemmed from early childhood trauma, particular sexual trauma. Such women sought emotional intensity rather than relational intimacy, which frequently led to sexual addiction or serial cheating. Sharon likely had deep underlying issues she wasn't addressing, and their marriage had suffered as a result.

Stanton casually strolled through the living room. Draped over a white sofa was the hide of a snow leopard, white with black spots. He ran his hand over the soft fur, entwining his fingers in the hair, before he stepped away and went into the study, which held shelves and shelves of books and a computer with two monitors. The desk was old mahogany, and gold and silver pens glimmered in the sunlight. Stanton took in the entire space before he walked through to the kitchen, looked in the fridge, then made his way upstairs to the master bedroom.

He stood still, watching dust swirl in beams of light. The house was quiet and empty. Richard wasn't here. In the bathroom, Stanton took a seat on the edge of the tub. Beginning in one corner, he ran his eyes along the baseboards and up the walls, all the way to the bathtub behind him.

The spatters of blood were still on the carpet. SIS had determined that someone was backing out of the closet after being injured. But injured with what? No weapon had been found. He rose and went through the closest, checking anything that could cause a person's nose to bleed from impact. Shoes, belts, and even a heavy watch could do it. But nothing seemed out of place. He stepped into the bathroom again.

Stanton looked up at the ceiling and down the shower to the rod. On the corner farthest away from him was a blemish. Balancing on the edge of the tub, he inspected the blemish on the curtain rod. A black stain over a dent. He took out his cell phone, focused the camera on the dent, then enhanced the image five times.

The shower rod had a nick in it, as though it had made an impact with something. The rod itself was just a little off center on the corners. A bit of mildew poked out as if the rod had been taken off and replaced in not quite the exact spot it'd been in before.

He twisted the rod slowly but didn't see any blood. Lifting it up, he could see the indentation and nick clearly from the top. But who would replace it? An intruder who'd been struck hard enough to bleed certainly wouldn't take the time to replace the rod. Someone did it after.

He took a few photos of the rod then put it back. Someone had replaced the rod after coming upon the scene but hadn't cleaned up the blood. This person had wanted the police to find the blood and the ski mask but not the misplaced rod. Or perhaps someone had simply put the rod back in its place without thinking it was part of the crime scene because the dent was small enough to miss.

Stanton had a guess as to who that person was.

22

Stanton arrived at the offices of Strain, Klep & Barnum a little after one o'clock. On the way, he'd grabbed a puka dog—a hot dog drowning in various fruit juices—and a Diet Coke for lunch. He was sipping his drink as he approached the receptionist and smiled.

"Hi, Richard Miller, please."

"May I tell him who's here to see him?"

"Jon Stanton." He took a seat in the waiting area. The office was all glass, chrome, and white carpets—the type of place corporations came to hire an attorney. Few individuals, he figured, could afford the hourly rate the place charged. And the name seemed familiar... Klep. That was Sharon Miller's maiden name. Sharon Klep.

Richard came out to meet him, dressed in what Stanton guessed was a suit and watch that cost more than his Jeep. Richard's hair was perfectly neat, and his nails appeared freshly manicured.

"Did you get a manicure?" Stanton asked.

"Excuse me?"

"Your nails are glossy. Did you get a manicure?"

He cleared his throat. "No. Who would do that when his wife and child are missing?"

"Some people would surprise you."

"Yeah, I guess they would. What can I do for you, Detective? I'm a very busy man."

"I'm sure. I didn't want to take up much of your time. I just wanted to ask you if you moved anything in your home before calling the police."

"Like what?"

"A shower rod, for example."

Richard hesitated. "No. I saw the blood and called you guys immediately."

"Did anyone else move the rod?"

"No, and what the hell is this about? You should be out there looking for who kidnapped my wife, and instead, you're here asking me about shower rods."

Stanton grinned as if he were embarrassed. "Of course. I shouldn't waste your time with such trivial things."

"Thank you. Now please let me know if there are any updates."

"I will." Stanton turned away. "Oh, one thing—you never mentioned that your father-in-law was a founding partner of this firm."

"Does it matter?"

"No, not unless you two were to divorce, right? Because I don't think any father-in-law would keep around an ex-husband. But if something that wasn't your fault happened to your wife, that might be a different story."

Stanton hadn't initially wanted to reveal his hand by letting Richard know that he was the target of his investigation. But Richard was so anxious, so on edge and ready to explode, that Stanton needed to push him over that edge. Anger and panic were the two worst emotions human beings could feel. They crowded out all other emotions, and people who were angry or panicked made mistakes. Their rational thinking couldn't function properly.

"Just what the hell are you saying?" Richard said loudly. "That I had something to do with my wife's disappearance?"

"Did you?"

Richard's face flushed red. "I think it's time for you to get the hell outta my office. And don't come back here."

Stanton nodded. "Of course, I meant no insult. I'll call you with any updates, Mr. Miller."

"You better."

Stanton marched to the elevator and took out his cell phone. He marked the time: 1:27 p.m. He called Laka.

"Hey, I was just going to call you," she said.

"We need a warrant on Richard Miller's phone."

"Wow, that was quick. What's the PC?"

Stanton hesitated. He wondered if he was crossing a line, but a young girl was out there in the hands of people who clearly didn't value human life. He didn't see that he had a choice. "That's the thing. I don't think I have probable cause, not really. We need a judge that is happy with ambiguous."

"I think I know the judge from my days in Vice. Text me over the probable cause statement, and I'll see what I can do."

Stanton sat at the bullpen until the evening, catching up on paperwork from several other cases he had been neglecting. One involved the body of a man found in a swimming pool one morning by the occupants of the home after a party the night before. The autopsy report had just come back. The man had enormously high levels of opiates in his system. He had likely stumbled into the pool and drowned.

It was well past six o'clock when Laka stepped into the precinct detectives' offices. She strode straight over to Stanton and laid a document across his keyboard. It was a warrant for Richard Miller's phone records.

"Wow," he said. "I'm impressed."

"I'm impressed you wanted to get his records with so little."

He shrugged. "He had something to do with this. But he's in over his head and doesn't know what to do next. I get the impression of a rat lost in a maze when I see him."

"What're you looking for in the phone records?"

"I want to see who he called after I left. I pushed him, and I bet he panicked. Just a guess. I could be wrong, so I hope you didn't burn any bridges getting this warrant."

"Not at all. Judge Anderson loves me."

"Well," Stanton said, stretching his arms over his head, "let's get this to the phone company."

23

Dark and filled with smoke, the bar was the type of place a man like Richard Miller wouldn't be caught in a million years. The dance floor was in back, and a mirror hung over the bar, one of the bars anyway. Another one was on the second floor. The acute lack of women was noticeable. The clientele wanted to get drunk, not pick up girls. Richard only went there late at night, and he dressed so that no one he knew would recognize him.

But at that moment, he didn't care if anyone noticed him. He was wearing his two-thousand-dollar suit with the pocket square, his hair was just perfect, and his shoes were so shiny he could see his reflection in them. He sat at the bar on the second level, staring at the empty dance floor.

The beer he'd been nursing for the past half hour was nearly gone, and he motioned to the bartender for another. The bartender, a well-built man with a sleeveless shirt, slid the beer over to him and leaned forward.

"You're usually happy to see me, Rich."

"I'm just not feeling it today. One of those days, I guess."

"What happened? Mrs. Miller again?"

"Yeah, basically. You ever felt like the world was a tuxedo, and you were a brown pair of shoes, David? 'Cause that's what I'm feeling right about now."

"Well, cheer up. Tomorrow's always another day."

"Yeah, there's that, I suppose." He swigged a few gulps of his new beer. "Were you ever married, David?"

"Nope," he said, wiping the counter with a fresh rag. "Never saw the point. You don't eat the same breakfast cereal every morning. Why would you want to wake up next to the same person every morning?"

"Makes sense, I guess."

David put his elbows on the bar and looked Richard in the eyes. "You really love her, don't you?"

He nodded. "Despite everything I feel and all the terrible things that have happened, deep down, I love her."

"Then what are you doing in here? Go be with her."

He swallowed. "I did something terrible, David."

His brow furrowed. "This does sound serious. What did you do?"

"I—"

Richard felt his cell phone vibrate in his pocket and took it out. The call was from a number he didn't recognize, so he let it go to voicemail.

"Sorry," he said.

"No worries. So what did you do?"

He downed some beer. Before he could answer, he received a text message. All it said was, "You want to talk to me about Sharon. Call me."

"Sorry, David. I better take this."

"Sure, we can talk later."

When David was out of earshot, Richard called the number. It rang twice before a man with a high-pitched voice answered.

"This Richard Miller?"

"Yes. Who am I speaking with?" Richard had to plug his other ear with his finger to hear.

"You don't know me, but I know you. I know Tate, too. And the thing with your wife. I got your number from his phone."

Richard's heart dropped into his stomach. "What do you want?"

"Tate isn't going to kill her, man. He went out and bought a bunch of fake blood an' shit to send you a pic."

"Well, what's he gonna do?"

"He's gonna sell 'em. Both of 'em."

"What do you mean *sell* them? To who?"

"To some pimp, man. He's gonna turn your wife and daughter out. Then they get shuffled around from city to city for a while. If they fine enough, they get moved overseas. Arab countries and shit. Them camel jockeys love white girls."

Though no one else could hear the conversation, Richard glanced around. Everyone was busy in their own groups, not paying any attention to him. "What are you talking about?"

"I told you, man. He's gonna sell your wife and daughter. We're talkin' slavery, man."

"How do you know this?"

"'Cause I'm right here with him. But you know, it's the true man that takes that extra step to make somethin' of himself. You know?"

"I don't understand. If you're with him, why are you calling me?"

The man sighed. "You as stupid as a rock, ain't you? I want money. All of it. Everything you were payin' Tate to me. And I get your daughter back for you. I don't think you give a shit about your wife."

"Well, no, no, I want them both back. Get them both back for me, and I'll get you your money. Every penny."

"You hired us to—"

"I know what I hired you for, but I want them both back now. Unharmed."

He was silent a beat. "Okay, but none of this escrow shit. I want a bag with cash, and we do a trade."

"Okay, fine, whatever."

"Gimme some time, and I'll call you back when I got 'em."

The line went silent. Richard stared at the screen. He quickly programmed the number into his contacts. Then he sighed and placed the phone down on the bar, staring at it. "David, better get me a vodka and cranberry juice. Don't think I'm going home for a while."

24

Evening fell over the island, and the sun began its descent into the ocean as Stanton watched from a window at the phone company. The manager was in the middle of dinner with his family, and he did not seem pleased to get the call to come in for the records.

The manager stomped by them then glanced back. "You the cops?"

"Yes."

"Be out in a minute," he groaned.

Forty-five minutes later, they were still waiting. Stanton guessed the manager could've retrieved the information a lot faster, but he wanted to make them wait as punishment for missing dinner. Laka had been occupied by her phone the entire time.

"You don't have to stay, you know," he said.

"I'm your partner. That's what partners do, right?"

He grinned. "Did you have a partner in Vice?"

"No, we worked in teams, so there really wasn't any need. We'd set up underage drinking stings, prostitution, stuff like that. Kai told me you've never worked Vice. You didn't really strike me as the type."

"And what type would that be?"

"Those guys are crazy. Some of them get blowjobs from the hookers before we bust them, get drunk at parties when they're there to make a collar, stuff like that." She glanced up at him and put down her phone. "I can tell by the way you're looking at me that you don't approve."

"I tell everybody that I bust that if you keep clear of trouble, trouble will keep clear of you. Think of it as a law of nature, I guess. That works on this side of the law, too. Eventually, people will find out how they behave. There'll be investigations, Vice will be disbanded and spread to other units, and every case they have ever worked will be under suspicion. I've seen it before."

"With Barlow."

He nodded. "His corruption ran deep. He used the police force as his personal army. But it's the same principle. The only way to avoid bad things happening to you is to avoid the situations that bring those things about."

"I'm not sure they see it that way. I think they see it as harmless fun."

"We have the authority to arrest and even kill civilians. We have to take that seriously. Fun shouldn't be part of it."

The manager opened his office door. He grumbled something under his breath and handed Stanton a USB drive along with a stack of documents. "All his phone records for the past two months."

"I appreciate it. Thank you."

The manager stormed out without saying anything further. He waited for them by the door, holding it open.

"I think he's gonna lock us in if we don't leave," Laka said.

They rose, and Stanton flipped through the papers as they rode the elevator down in silence, listening to the soft music.

Laka checked her phone and grinned at Stanton. "Looks like you hurt someone's feelings," she said.

"Who?"

"Debbie. She said you were going to go out with them and never showed up."

"I completely forgot about that. I thought it was just kind of a pity invite."

"No, definitely not. She's into you."

Stanton, despite himself, thought he was blushing. The manager looked to him and rolled his eyes.

Once they were in his Jeep, Stanton immediately flipped to the phone records for the current day and searched all the calls Richard made after they'd spoken at one o'clock.

At 1:29, two minutes after Stanton had visited Richard, he'd placed a call to a local number. Stanton called into the precinct and asked for Records.

"Records," Harold Finks mumbled.

"Harold, this is Jon Stanton. I need a number run if you have the time, please."

He exhaled loudly. "Fine, what's the number?"

Stanton read it to him. He heard keys being pressed on a keyboard, then Harold said, "It's registered to a Tate Reynolds. Residence here on the island. Looks like he had an address in Los Angeles before that."

"Can you text me the address, Harold? And any relatives that pop up?"

"You want a criminal history to save you a Spillman search?"

"I would. Thank you."

"I'll send that over."

"I really appreciate it."

"Well, you've always said *please*."

Stanton placed the phone down on the center console. He looked at Laka. "He called a number after I left him. Tate Reynolds. Harold's getting me his address and criminal history."

She finished sending a text. "Well, I'm starving. Can we get some dinner while we wait?"

Stanton parked at the curb in front of Sushi Gaku on King Street. He hopped out of the Jeep and met Laka at the back. A group of young men walking by on the sidewalk stared at her as they passed, impressed by her figure, her tight shirt, or the gold badge clipped to her waistband. Power was an aphrodisiac for men, too.

The restaurant was busy, but he and Laka didn't have to wait long. They sat at a window booth, and Stanton turned his phone on vibrate then placed it in his pocket. Laka set hers on the table. They were certainly from different generations. Stanton hadn't grown up with cell phones, and she had.

"Can I ask you something?" she said.

"Sure."

"You have a PhD in psychology, right?"

"I do."

"Why in the hell are you a cop?"

"I think I always knew I would be going into law enforcement of some kind. I thought the doctorate would help me in that."

"Were you thinking FBI?"

"I have a lot of friends in the FBI, and I was offered a spot with them. I turned it down."

"Wow, really? Most cops dream of going federal."

He shook his head. "There's something about the way they garner power. Illegal phone taps, reading people's e-mails without a warrant—something about it strikes me as dangerous. I don't think I'd fit in well there."

"We didn't have much to get a warrant on Miller."

"We worked the system by finding a judge that would agree with us. It wasn't my proudest moment, and maybe I shouldn't have done it, but it's a far cry from arresting someone under the Patriot Act and holding them without an attorney for weeks at a time."

She looked out the window. "I never thought I'd be a cop. I thought it'd be more the opposite when I was young. I ran with a gang and was smoking pot and getting drunk every night. This was when I was like seventeen."

"What changed?"

Her countenance transformed as though an unwelcome memory had flashed through her mind. "I, um, was running with some bad people. And they did something that… I just didn't think people were capable of."

"What?"

"No offense, but we haven't known each other that long."

"I understand. I didn't mean anything by it. I was just curious."

"No, I shouldn't be so secretive. I just haven't ever told anyone."

The waiter came and took their orders. Stanton's phone vibrated in his pocket as the waiter asked him if they needed one ticket or two.

"One, please," he said, taking out his phone. Harold had sent a text with an attached document—Tate Reynolds's criminal history.

The history read like a textbook on a permanently revolving-door prisoner. He began in property crimes, like car theft and robbery, as a juvenile and had graduated to crimes against persons by the time he was seventeen. He had several convictions for aggravated assault, and his longest stint in prison—eight years—had been for rape. But two charges that had been dismissed interested Stanton the most. Twelve years ago, Tate had been charged twice with kidnapping. There were no notes indicating why they had been dismissed.

"We need to go pay Tate Reynolds a visit," Stanton said.

"Can we eat first?"

Stanton wanted to get over there, but he placed his phone down and said, "Sure. We'll eat first."

25

Tate Reynolds was smoking a bowl outside of Lee's house on the large patio stacked with furniture. A few neighbors were out, but they were also getting high or getting drunk to be able to get through another day.

Tate sprinkled a fine white powder on his weed. Angel dust. He'd started experimenting with it in high school when he was running with a biker gang. One of his buddies had ripped out his own eyeball while he was on the stuff, and since then, Tate had been careful. He only sprinkled it on his weed. The drug's effects were powerful and immediate. He felt as if he could stop a semi-truck with his body or jump off a building and break through the cement like Superman. But it left a bad taste in his mouth, as though he'd eaten a light bulb.

Tate finished the bowl just as a car pulled up to the house—a Rolls-Royce Phantom that Tate was certain cost almost half a million dollars. Three men, all black, were inside. Two were beefy guys dressed in sports coats, with gold chains dangling from their necks. The one in the backseat was wearing a fedora, a purple suit, and matching shoes. He stepped out with a golden cup in his hand and gave it to the guy in the passenger seat then approached the home.

"Where's Lee?" he demanded.

Tate shouted, "Lee, get out here."

Lee stumbled out a second later. "Hey, Dominic. What's up, man? Where you been?"

"Here and there, little cuz. How's your mama?"

"She good. Gettin' by, you know."

"That's good. Well, you tell her hello for me."

"I will."

Tate blew out a puff of smoke. "So, we gonna do business, or you guys gonna suck each other's dicks the whole time?"

Dominic stared at him. He turned back to Lee and asked, "Who's this arrogant muthafucka?"

"It's Tate, man. The one I told you about on the phone."

"Fuck this muthafucka. I don't do business with cocky-ass cracker Nazi muthafuckas."

"No, Dominic, he's cool. I know him from back in the day. He just got some bitches and wanted to meet you."

Dominic turned to Tate. "That right, cracka? You got some bitches you want me to look at?"

Tate placed the pipe down on the side table and rose to his feet. "I didn't think pimps were supposed to dress like pimps. Don't that make the cops come lookin' at you?"

"You gotta dress for tha game if you gonna be in tha game. Where them bitches?"

Tate motioned toward the RV. Dominic strode over there, and Tate and Lee followed. When no one was looking, Tate reached back and felt the grip of his pistol. He didn't trust any of those fools. They could all turn on him. As far as he knew, Lee was playing him.

Dominic opened the door to the RV and stepped inside. Hiapo was sitting at the table. The young girl was on the bed.

"The older one's in the bathroom," Tate said.

Dominic strolled into the back and opened the bathroom. Sharon was seated on the toilet. Though she didn't look as hot as she had the night before, her beauty still shone through. Dominic looked her over like a farmer examining a cow.

"What... what are you going to do with me?" she stammered.

"Nothin', baby doll," he said. He turned to Eliza. For her, a smile came over his lips. "How old are you, child?"

"Thirteen."

"Thirteen. And I bet you ain't never been with a boy, have you? You ain't never fucked?"

She shook her head.

"That's a good girl. You save yourself. That's valuable. Most valuable thing a bitch has." He watched her a moment longer then sauntered back to the front of the RV. When he walked, he tried to appear as though he were gliding with a limp. It was too much. The pimps he'd known were just junkies who raped and beat girls often enough to get the girls to work for them. That meant either Dominic was so high level that Tate had never seen a pimp like him, or he was full of shit and posing as one.

"I'll give you twenty-five hundred for both," Dominic said.

Tate scoffed. "You asked about her fuckin' 'cause you know virgins is worth a lot, don't you? And I can turn them out myself and make twenty-five in a weekend. I'm talkin' about selling 'em off."

"And who else you gonna sell 'em bitches to, cracka? You ain't know nobody. And you put them bitches on the street without any experience in tha game, and some other nigga gonna steal them bitches in a minute." He looked at Lee and exhaled. "But if you a friend of my cousin's, then I be straight with you. Virgins bring in a lot. Some folks pay as much as twenty-five G's to be with a virgin her age. I can get her overseas to them Muslim muthafuckas and make even more. The other one's just a whore like any other. Ain't worth much. But I take the girl."

"No, you take 'em both. I don't want either of 'em."

Dominic thought a moment, staring at his freshly manicured fingernails on his left hand. "A'ight. I give you fifteen for the both of them. And that's it."

"I can live with fifteen."

Dominic nodded and stuck out his hand. Tate slowly put out his hand and took the other man's palm.

"Gimme one day to get the money to you."

"A day? Player like you doesn't have fifteen K laying around?"

"Have to have untraceable bills. I don't write muthafuckin' checks."

Dominic said good-bye to his cousin and stepped off the RV. Tate watched him go, a grin on the pimp's face. He took out a cigarette and lit it, turning to Hiapo, who was also grinning. "Hundred and fifteen K, and I didn't have to hurt either of 'em. You see that, Lee? That's how you get shit done."

"Cool, man. And I get a taste, right?"

"You get two K for callin' your cousin."

"Two K? Y'all parked in front of my house. You couldn't've done this without me."

"Two K. You got a problem with that?"

Lee swallowed and looked from Hiapo to Tate. "Nah, man." He turned and opened the door without another word.

When Lee had left the RV, Tate sat down at the table and slapped Hiapo's shoulder. He smoked a bit more then said, "Where the fuck is Sticks?"

26

Stanton was acquainted with this section of the island. But he'd never been there at night, so nothing looked familiar. Fences, which were falling down, surrounded rundown homes. Dogs were chained up in a few torn-up lawns. Several cars that he knew wouldn't run were parked on the block. There was no HOA there, not even much of a police presence unless someone was raped or murdered.

Tate Reynolds lived in a brown one-story home with no fence. A group of young men were drinking in front, near the corner of an intersection. As he rode by in his Jeep, he heard two of them say, "Po-po, man."

Even though he was in his Jeep, wearing casual clothing, they could somehow tell. Just like most cops had a sixth sense when it came to criminals, they had a sixth sense about the cops, too. Stanton parked in front of the house and got out. Laka pulled her jacket out of the backseat and put it on, covering as much flesh as possible. As they walked up the sidewalk, the men stepped back without saying anything. Stanton looked them over to make sure no one was reaching for a weapon. The men eyed him, staring him down, but didn't go for anything.

The screen door was falling off its hinges. Stanton pulled it back carefully and knocked. A light went on inside the house. Slowly, the lock turned, and he could hear a chain being pulled off the metal latch. The door opened, and just the slightest hint of a young woman thrust part of her face out, only her eyes and forehead.

"Yes?" she said quietly.

"I'm looking for Tate Reynolds. Is he here?"

"No."

"Do you know where he is?"

"No."

Stanton looked back at the men on the corner. They were listening to everything. "We're with the Honolulu Police Department. May we come inside, please?"

She hesitated. "I guess."

She opened the door, and Stanton stepped in first. The house had no furniture other than an old futon covered with blankets and pillows in the living room and a beat-up table in the kitchen.

"What's your name, ma'am?"

"Cindy." She folded her arms across her chest.

"We just need to talk to Tate. I think he may be involved with some bad people, and he doesn't know what's going on."

"Tate can take care of himself," she said.

"I'm sure he can. But I'd like to speak with him anyway. Any idea when he'll be back?"

She shook her head.

"Have you talked to him recently?"

"Yesterday."

"I take it you're his girlfriend," Laka said.

"No, his wife."

Stanton glanced around the home. He could picture their entire marriage, nothing but drugs and abuse. The track marks going up Cindy's arms told him she was a prisoner there, just as if she'd been chained in the basement. Her old bruises had healed over, only to be bruised again. She was terrified and confused.

"Tate left you here by yourself," he said. "He doesn't care about you. You don't owe him anything."

She stared at the floor. "He takes care of me."

"He uses you. Nothing else. I know someone that can get you out of here. Get you a place to stay until you find a job and land on your feet."

She looked up at him. "Away from here?"

"Cindy, you don't have to be here. He doesn't own you."

For an instant, and only an instant, a hope flashed across her face. Her eyes lit up, and her lips parted as though she were about to smile. But as quickly as it had come, the hope faded away. And her eyes sank back to the floor. "I don't know nothin'," she mumbled.

Stanton watched her for a moment. "Where did he say he was going?"

Cindy shrugged.

"Who is he with?"

"Sticks and H."

"H?"

"Hiapo. I don't know his last name. They stopped here and got some things and left again."

"Do you know Sticks's name?"

"His first name's Tom. I don't know his last name."

Stanton glanced around once more. "Are you sure you don't want to take me up on that offer, Cindy?"

She nodded.

"Mind if I have a quick look around?"

She didn't say anything, so Stanton walked into the kitchen then the bedroom. He was looking for a basement or attic, somewhere Tate may have hidden something. But the house's few rooms were bare.

As he and Laka left, Stanton saw the young men on the corner. They had been watching the house the entire time. He had no doubt that they would relay everything they'd heard to Tate as soon as they saw him.

"I can run the AKA Sticks through Spillman," Laka said. "Might get lucky. It's kind of unique."

"Do it. I'm going to hit another source."

"What source?"

"Just a guy I know."

27

The bar and grill wasn't really a bar, and it definitely wasn't a grill. Stanton had never been there in person. Whenever he needed something from the owner, he called. The owner was a squat, obese man named Billy Green. Because his name was so close to the Michael Jackson song, people called him "Jean." When Stanton stepped inside, he saw Jean waddle into the back.

The bar was hazy with cigarette and weed smoke. It catered mostly to bikers and drug dealers, but sometimes, average citizens looking for a cheap prostitute went there, too. The biker gangs had jumped on prostitution once they figured out that the cops weren't enforcing the laws against it anymore. Most of their girls had been taken from pimps the gang members had beaten or killed, but some had been kidnapped. Some were runaways, and others were bought and sold like cattle.

For their first year or so, most of the girls tried to run for help. So the gangs kept the new girls on lockdown for the first year. They brought the johns in to see the men, and the girls weren't allowed outside by themselves. After the first year, Stockholm Syndrome would begin to wear away their will to be free, and they began to form false relationships with their captors and willingly accepted their positions as sex slaves.

Stanton saw the girls. He had covered up his badge and left his gun locked in a hidden compartment of the Jeep. He hoped that was enough to prevent anyone from recognizing him as a cop at first glance. He got stares as he strolled through the bar, but nothing threatening. Someone like him being there was a normal occurrence. In fact, it was how they made their money. Men would get off work and stop here for a drink, a girl, or some blow before heading home to their wives, who had no idea what their husbands' private lives were like.

At the bar, Stanton waited for the bartender, a woman with tattoos running the length of her arms.

She looked at him without smiling. "Yeah, what did you want?"

"I need to talk to Jean, please."

"He's in back. I'll grab him when I get a sec."

"Sure. Thanks. Um, can I get an apple juice please?"

The woman gave him an odd look before pouring the juice. Not drinking would have been a sure sign that he was a police officer, and he hoped the apple juice looked just enough like whiskey or beer to avoid raising any suspicions.

After wiping down the bar and serving three beers to a table in the corner, the bartender went in back. A moment later, Jean hobbled out. He motioned with his head for Stanton to join him in back.

The back room was cluttered with paper and cartons of liquor. Jean cleared some space on a chair by folding the papers together and forcing them into a drawer. Stanton sat down across from him and waited until the man got up and shut the door. He took a flask from his pocket and swigged some whiskey before sitting back down and wiping his lips. "I don't like you coming here, Jon. As much as I like you."

"I wouldn't have if I didn't need to. Sometimes, you don't call me be back for a day or two, and this couldn't wait."

"Hm. Well, I appreciate you hiding your badge at least. What was it you needed?"

"I'm looking for someone with the nickname Sticks."

"Sticks, huh? Why you need him?"

"I think he's involved in a kidnapping and murder."

Jean whistled through his teeth and took another sip of the whiskey. Stanton could smell it. He knew the whiskey was the most expensive thing Jean imported. He wasn't one to skimp on booze.

"Yeah, I know him. He's low level. Nothin' but a punk. He and his buddy Tate come in here sometimes and sell their shit."

Stanton nodded, noticing a poster of a naked woman behind Jean. He immediately looked away. Jean and Stanton had an understanding. Stanton didn't inquire into the bar's activities, and Jean gave him information whenever he asked. Jean had been invaluable to numerous investigations. Where the police's information ended, Jean's began. It was worth letting the drug dealing slide. But Jean knew human trafficking was not something Stanton tolerated. If Stanton ever saw any direct evidence of it, he wouldn't hesitate to arrest him. Maybe one day, Stanton thought, he would. Right now, he needed him.

"I need to find him."

"He's usually over at the Red Buckle. You know the place?"

"Yeah, a bar down in Chinatown, right?"

"That's the one. His uncle or someone owns the place, so he's always there."

He nodded and rose. "I appreciate it, Jean. Take care of yourself."

"Yeah, man, well, see, you can actually do me somethin', too."

"What is it?"

"My little sister, man. She's locked up right now on a coke charge. Anything you can do?"

Stanton took out his phone and opened a note pad app. "What's her name?"

"Melinda Green."

"I'll see what I can do."

As he was on his way out, one of the women stepped in front of Stanton with a wry smile on her face. She placed a finger in one of his belt buckles, exposing his badge that was clipped to his belt. She saw it. "Interested?"

"No thank you," he said.

She slipped her finger out of the buckle and walked to the bar. As he opened the door to step outside, he heard her say, "Fag." He didn't miss a beat as he shut the door and walked to his Jeep. He wanted to get to Chinatown as quickly as possible. Even with a gun and a badge, he didn't want to be there alone too late at night.

28

The person in the mirror didn't even look like him anymore. There were wrinkles where there hadn't been any before, his hairline was pulling back, and his stomach was pushing out. Richard Miller thought he looked much more like his biological father than the picture he had of himself in his head.

He splashed cold water on his face and stared at himself again, hoping the image of his father had washed away. But it was still there, glaring at him and mocking him. Thinking of his real father made him think of the man who'd raised him—and judged him—his entire life. The connection brought back a memory he thought he'd forgotten. Prom. One of the most painful nights of his life. Not only had his date, Lauren Howell, only gone out with him because her sister, who was dating his brother, had forced her to go, but while Richard was waiting for her in her living room, he'd also heard her parents speaking. Her father told her mother that Richard's father had called to say that Richard was a runt, and he would be happy to have one of his other, better sons go with Lauren.

Richard's father had hated him his entire life, and he had never known why—until a few years before his father's death. His older brother Chad had informed Richard that he was not actually their father's son. He was the product of his mother's affair with a neighbor. They'd kept it secret, so as not to shame the family, and tried to raise Richard as their own.

He'd only gotten to know his father—his real father—for a few years. He had lived in a studio apartment and was a full-blown alcoholic. Richard had only known him twenty minutes before the man had hit him up for money. And the most frightening part was that Richard looked just like him now. The vision of a future that might have been terrified him to his core.

Richard wiped the water from his face with a paper towel just as someone walked into the bar's bathroom. He watched the man's reflection in the mirror. Daniel something. He was a club kid, though he was probably in his early thirties.

"Hey," Daniel said.

"Hey."

"Rich, right?"

"Yeah."

"Cool, man."

Daniel opened one of the stalls and stepped inside. He leaned against the wall and took out a small vial. He placed a little bit of white powder on his hand then snorted it in one nostril followed by the other.

"You want?" Daniel asked, wiping the edges of his nostrils with his fingertips.

"Um, well, I've never actually done it."

"You'll love it, man."

Richard stepped over and stood in the stall with the man, leaning against the opposite wall.

"Hold out your hand," Daniel said.

Richard did as he was told. Daniel tapped the vial against the back of Richard's hand. Some of the powder came out onto his skin.

"Just stick your nose over it and snort."

Richard did that, too. It burned going up, and he suddenly felt as though his sinuses were plugged. He had the overwhelming urge to blow his nose.

"How's it feel?"

"Well…"

The rush came as though he'd jumped off a cliff. The impact was palpable. Fire coursed through him, his heart raced, and suddenly, nothing seemed so bad. "Wow, that is… Wow!"

"Yeah." Daniel chuckled. He took a snort then offered more to Richard, who sucked it all up.

"This is good stuff," Richard bellowed, standing a little taller.

"It's average. Cut with baby laxative. But if you do a lot of it, the shit'll hit the spot."

Richard did another snort and shook his head. He felt a hundred feet tall. He started bobbing his head even though he could barely hear the music through the thick bathroom walls. His phone rang, and he didn't recognize the sound right away. Then he dipped into his pocket.

"Excuse me," Richard said, hopping out of the stall and going to stand by the urinals. "This is Richard."

"Hey, so they selling the bitches tomorrow. The guy needs a day to get the money together. I'm gonna get 'em tonight. Can you have the money?"

"Yeah, yeah, I can have the cash in the morning."

"Get it now. I'll tell you where to meet me."

"It's gotta be in the morning. The money's in the bank, and they're not open."

Richard caught a glimpse of himself in the mirror as he hung up his phone. He was still the alcoholic he'd seen in the filthy apartment. But he didn't care as much anymore.

"You got more, Daniel?" he asked loudly.

"Yeah, man. What's mine is yours."

29

Stanton knew Chinatown well. It was the one place every tourist was told not to go. Tour guides advised to visit during the day if the trip was unavoidable, and even then, the morning was best, before everyone was up.

Two months prior, three assailants had gunned a man down in the middle of the street, using assault rifles with hollow-point bullets. The Chinatown drug dealers had nothing to fear from the police because they were better armed than the department was.

Stanton parked in the lot behind the Red Buckle. A neon sign hung over the front door, and the back entrance was boarded up. He walked around front after checking then holstering his weapon.

The interior was in shambles. The bar looked as though it were a hundred years old and hadn't been cleaned since it first opened its doors. The floors were stained, and the tables were more so. One cocktail waitress and a bartender saw to the entire space, with two bouncers by the door smoking cigarettes. The bouncers' shirts bulged with hidden weapons.

No one checked his ID as he entered and walked casually up to the bar. He had no photograph of Sticks, so he sat at the bar and watched. The bartender didn't ask if he needed anything. When Stanton placed a twenty down, the bartender came over, and he ordered a virgin margarita. Suddenly, he felt foolish for ordering an apple juice before when he could've just done that.

He glanced around at the booths. None of them were lighted, so it was difficult to tell who was there. Two pool tables were in back, and he could hear the crack of the cue ball against the others. He waited patiently for a few minutes, until the bartender was near him.

"Sticks here tonight?" he asked.

The bartender eyed him. "You a friend of his?"

"Actually, I owe him some money, and he told me he might be here tonight."

The bartender turned to another customer who was yelling his order. "He's in back at the tables," he said, without turning back to Stanton.

Stanton pushed the drink away and rose. As he turned toward the tables, a large man in a ripped T-shirt bumped into him.

"Watch it, asshole."

"Sorry," Stanton said.

"You fuckin' made me spill my drink."

"How about another one on me?" He motioned to the bartender. He wasn't thinking clearly. Sticks was in back, and he just wanted past this guy. If his thoughts had been clear, he would've known that backing down as quickly as he had was a sign of weakness. He'd spilled blood in the water with this group of sharks.

"Fuck you, cocksucker," the man said, pushing him back.

A few people turned around, curious as to what was about to go down.

Stanton smiled. "No harm intended. Let me pay for your next few rounds, and we'll call it good."

"How 'bout I bash your fucking face in, and we call it good."

The bartender chimed in. "Leave him alone, Hank. He owes money to Sticks. Let the man pay his bill."

Hank spit a putrid mix of snot and chewing tobacco on Stanton's shoes. Stanton stepped around him, and Hank didn't do anything.

The back room was just two pool tables and an unplugged jukebox. A man and a woman were at one of the tables. The woman was dressed scantily, and dark circles hung under her eyes. The man had greasy hair and torn jeans. His face was weathered as though he'd spent a lifetime in the sun. They both looked up as Stanton walked in.

"Are you Sticks?" Stanton asked.

For a silent moment, Sticks kept his eyes on Stanton, who didn't move.

In a burst of movement, Sticks threw the pool stick at Stanton and tossed the girl to the floor near Stanton's feet. The girl screamed as Sticks sprinted out the back. Stanton dashed after him, jumped over the girl, and rushed through the back door.

Sticks raced through the parking lot. Stanton was right behind him, pumping his arms to keep up. Sticks jumped the fence separating the bar from the carpet outlet next door. Stanton followed. He thrust one foot into the fence and used it as leverage to hoist himself over. Sticks was on the other side, pulling a gun from his waistband.

Stanton hit the ground and rolled, coming up with his Desert Eagle pointed at the man's heart. Sticks didn't even have his gun out yet. He turned and ran.

Stanton, with the gun at his side, chased him around the store into the street. They emerged onto the main road, running across old, out-of-service train tracks. Sticks was panting and wheezing. Stanton didn't feel anything but a burning in his thighs.

They sprinted up the tracks to an empty field. Sticks was slowing down. His breathing was getting louder and wetter, as though he might have been foaming at the mouth. He lifted the pistol behind him and fired.

The round went wide. Instead of stopping, Stanton ducked his head and pumped his legs for all they had. He slammed into Sticks at the waist, and another bullet passed so close to Stanton's ear that he was certain he would've heard the buzz if the pop hadn't deafened him.

The two men hit the ground so hard that they both grunted as they rolled over the tracks. Stanton held on tightly to Sticks's clothing, making sure the gun couldn't get near him. When they stopped rolling, Stanton grabbed the man's right arm, his firing arm. He twisted like a snake, pinning Sticks's arm in the crook of his thighs, holding tightly to the man's wrist. His Desert Eagle lay in the dirt, out of reach.

Stanton pulled back with everything he had and heard the soft crack of Sticks's elbow. The man howled in pain. Stanton rolled on top of him into the Gracie mount, with his legs wrapped around Sticks's waist and one hand to his throat. Both guns were in the dirt now.

Sticks rolled onto his back, a classic mistake for someone in the Gracie mount. Stanton wrapped his arm around Sticks's throat and pulled up, cutting off his air. Sticks gurgled and went limp after only a few seconds. Stanton waited until he felt the man weaken underneath him, then he loosened his arm enough for Sticks to breathe. He squeezed again, as hard as he could, cutting off the air, just to show him he could. Then he loosened his grip again.

"Where's Sharon Miller and the girl?" Stanton asked, breathing hard.

"Fuck you."

Stanton squeezed again. His other arm was behind the head, pushing forward, and the two acted like scissors, cutting off the man's air. Stanton waited until Sticks nearly passed out.

"Where?"

"I don't have 'em."

"Who does? Tate?"

"Yeah, yeah, Tate has 'em. Go get him."

"Where is he?"

"Up your mother's cunt," Sticks said then laughed.

Stanton lifted him and slammed his head down, nearly knocking him unconscious. He pulled out his cuffs and slapped them on the man's wrists.

30

Tate paced the basement of Lee's house. He felt jittery, almost as if he were wearing the wrong skin. He'd called Sticks and told him what was up, and Sticks had said he would be right there. That was three hours ago. And he still hadn't come. The stupid asshole was probably high and shacked up with some girl. Sticks might not be out to Lee's house again in time for the trade. No biggie. Tate didn't plan on giving him a cut anyway. As far as he was concerned, the score was his money and no one else's.

He pulled out the last of his weed and slumped onto a couch. The shit was laced with so much angel dust that he couldn't smoke it. He tried to separate the weed and the angel dust on a table in front of him, but it wasn't working.

"Hey, Lee," he shouted. "You got any ganja?"

"Yeah, man. Hold up."

Tate stood and paced the room again. He tried to lay down on Lee's waterbed, but the wavy motion made him nauseated, and he rose and returned to his pacing. Lee came down a few minutes later, with a bong and some weed.

They sat at the table, and Lee lit up a bowl and took a hit before passing it over. Tate took three or four lungfuls and seemed to melt into the chair. Each of his muscles instantly felt loose and relaxed. He took another pull then passed it on.

"You gotta take it easy on this shit," Lee said. "Primo stuff, baby."

"Your cousin, he a real pimp? Or he a fake-ass bitch?"

"Nah, man. Dominic been in the game since he was a young kid. Started with his girlfriend back when he was fifteen, man. You believe that? Nigga was fifteen and turnin' bitches out. He went away for a while, though, but that didn't do nothin'. He came out, and he wasn't scared of nobody no more. But he don't really pimp, though. He just get bitches and turn 'em out and then sell 'em off. It pays, and he ain't got to be out on the street every day." He took a pull off the bong and let it rest on the table as he blew circles of smoke into the air. "You been inside, too, though. What was that like?"

"You never been?"

"Nah, man. I ain't been busted for nothin' but DUI an' shit."

"It's crazy, man. Different planet." Tate took another pull from the bong, deep and burning. The weed calmed him enough that he almost thought he could sleep. "You got everyone split up by race, and they don't trust each other. But it's all bullshit 'cause you can't trust nobody in there anyway. People'll come up to you at first and be real nice. They'll bring you sandwiches and cookies and drinks. Some of 'em will bring you ganja and smoke with you. They act like your best friend. And then the second you need 'em, when you at your weakest and need somebody there, that's when they'll bite. Like some fucking cobra. And they'll take whatever you got. If you lucky, it's just your stuff."

"So, like, rapin' dudes? That happen to you?"

"Yeah, man. It happens to everyone in there. You either get punked, or you join up with your crew, your race. And some big dog there'll tell you that that's the price you gotta pay if you want protection. And sometimes, you just do it 'cause ain't no women around, and you get so lonely the world just don't make sense no more."

"Shit."

"Yeah, shit."

Tate's phone rang. He stared at it on the table and blinked slowly a couple of times before answering.

"Yeah?"

"Tate. This is Bridge, dog. My dipshit nephew with you?"

"I ain't seen Sticks since this mornin'. He took off. I called him, and he said he'd be down, but I ain't seen him."

"Well if you see him, tell him I need to talk to his ass. Some cop was down at Jean's askin' about him. Stopped up here, too. He and Sticks took off out the back, and ain't no one seen him since."

"What cop?"

"Shit if I know. But tell his stupid ass to call me."

"I will." Tate hung up and placed the phone down.

"What dat about?" Lee asked.

"I don't know. But I get the feelin' shit's hittin' the fan."

31

Interrogation Room Five was Stanton's favorite. It was farthest away from everyone else. It was bare, nothing but a gray table and two chairs. Even the carpet was simple gray and clean. He stared into the one-way glass and watched Sticks, whose real name was Thomas Nathan Cooper, though he had about a dozen aliases.

Sticks fidgeted and played with his fingers. He would twitch and run his fingers through his hair. He was obviously going through withdrawal.

Stanton glanced at Laka, who was standing behind him with her arms folded. "You should stay out here."

"Why?"

"He's weak. He'll try and impress you by fighting me on everything."

"If you say so. I think I can get the fucker to confess."

"How?"

"Womanly charms."

Stanton grinned. "Have at it."

Laka sauntered into the room and shut the door behind her. Sticks instantly perked up. Laka sat across from him. Stanton imagined what her pleasant smell must've been like for someone who probably hadn't showered in a week—probably arousing and soothing at once.

She flipped her hair and leaned back in the seat.

"How are you, Sticks?"

He grunted. "Where's that bitch-ass detective that almost broke my arm? I'm gonna sue his ass."

"*Almost* is the word. You just overextended your elbow. They didn't even put a cast on it. Where's your sling, by the way?"

"Don't need no fucking sling. What you want?"

She leaned forward, maintaining eye contact. "I'm interested in Sharon Miller. I just don't get how you're involved in this. The thing is, I know prison doesn't scare you. Nothing I can do can scare you, so I'm just going to be honest with you. I don't know why you would want to protect Tate. He doesn't care about you, from what I've heard."

"Heard from who?"

"His wife. She told us that he doesn't care about anyone but himself."

Stanton ran to the room and opened the door. "Detective, can I see you a minute?"

Laka rose and followed him out of the room. Stanton shut the door. He pulled her far enough away to ensure Sticks couldn't hear them.

"What's wrong?" she asked.

"You can't do that."

"What?"

"Blame Tate's wife. That makes her look like a snitch. They'll kill her for what you just said."

She looked at Sticks through the glass. "Shit. I just got excited. It just came out. I've never done that before."

Stanton turned to the glass and stared in. "We can't break him anyway. He's past the point of our reach. If prison really doesn't scare him, we don't have anything. But I bet I know who does."

The Red Buckle was busier near midnight. Unlike his previous trip, Stanton took along two uniformed officers, and his badge dangled from a chain around his neck. The atmosphere had changed. Conversations stopped. People stared at him as he walked by. One guy said, "You smell bacon, Jake?"

Stanton walked up to the bartender and said, "I need to see Sticks's uncle."

The bartender shouted, "Bridge, cops are here."

A door opened in the back, and a tall man in a white T-shirt stepped out. He stepped up behind the bar and placed both hands on it. "I help you, officers?"

The man was covered in prison tattoos that were only moderately hidden beneath his clothing. The most prominent was a swastika on his chest that thrust out of his low-neck shirt.

"Can we talk in private, please?"

Bridge nodded and led Stanton to a room in the back. Stanton told the officers to wait for him near the bar, followed Bridge inside, and shut the door. Bridge sat down in an executive chair and put his boots up on the desk. Stanton remained on his feet.

"All the permits are in order, officer."

"It's *detective*, actually. Jon Stanton, with the Honolulu PD homicide detail."

"So what can I do for you, *Detective*?"

"I know about the meth being sold out of this place. I spoke with the Narcs unit about it." He took a slip of paper out of his pocket and laid it on the desk in front of Bridge. "I have a warrant to search the premises, and I have six other officers waiting for me to call them so we can turn this place inside out."

Bridge's eyes slowly drifted up from the warrant to Stanton's eyes. "So? Why haven't you?"

"Because I was hoping we could help each other."

"And why would I want to help you?"

"Because you don't hide things as well as you think you do." Stanton leaned against the wall, placing one foot up on it. "The pool table, the first one, is slanted slightly to the right. I noticed it when I came to talk to Sticks earlier tonight. Almost like the table is filled with something that's making it uneven."

Bridge's face changed. He'd been in and out of prison his whole life, but he'd aged. Stanton guessed the man was pushing sixty. If he went back on a distribution charge, he would die in prison.

"What do you want?" Bridge asked softly.

"I want you to tell Sticks to give me the information I asked him for. I want Tate Reynolds. I think he killed a young boy, and I want to see him rotting in a cell for it. And I want the mother and daughter he kidnapped."

Bridge snorted. "What makes you think I can get Sticks to talk? That boy's more stubborn than a mule."

"You're his uncle. You can be persuasive when you need to be."

Bridge thought a moment then rose. "Lemme grab my jacket."

No one was near Interrogation Five when Stanton arrived. He and Bridge stared through the glass at Sticks, who was sweating so profusely that he had soaked his collar. His fingers trembled, and the slight twitch he'd had when Stanton had left had turned into a full spasm.

"Turn the camera off," Bridge said.

Stanton watched him for a second then reached over to a set of controls and switched off the camera. Bridge stepped into the room.

"Uncle Bridge," Sticks said, standing up, "I knew you'd get me out."

"We ain't goin' nowheres just yet, boy."

Sticks's face was priceless. Shock and confusion. Sticks was not used to fear, and Stanton knew he'd found the one man who could induce it in Sticks.

"Why ain't we leavin'?"

"'Cause I want you to tell that detective whatever he wants to know about Tate."

"What? Fuck that pig. I ain't tellin' him shit."

Bridge struck like a snake, grabbing the man's hair and slamming his head into the table. Sticks flew back, out of his chair. Every fiber in Stanton's body told him to go in there and end it. But then he remembered Adam Cummings lying in the bushes. And he saw Sharon and Eliza Miller the same way—bullets in their brains, lying alongside the road. He folded his arms and stepped away from the glass.

"What the fuck you doin'?" Sticks shouted.

"You stupid shit, you brought the whole fuckin' police force down on us. They got a warrant to search my place."

"I didn't know."

Bridge kicked Sticks in the gut, rolling him over. "You think I'm gonna die in the can 'cause of you? You gonna tell that detective what he wants to know, you hear me? Or I swear it, boy, I will cut your balls off and feed 'em to you. We clear?"

Another kick, this time in the chest, knocked the wind out of Sticks. He spat blood on the floor.

Stanton ran in. "That's enough."

"We clear?" Bridge asked.

Sticks sat up, wiping away the blood, his eyes wide. "We're clear."

Bridge nodded and looked at Stanton. "All yours."

32

· Richard was tired of being around people at the bar, so he left the bar and went home to an empty, dark house. He ate a frozen pizza for dinner and watched a sitcom in the unlit movie room in the basement, nibbling on cheese the entire time. Then he drank a glass of wine on his porch, hoping to run into a neighbor to speak with. But no one was out. No one ever came out.

So he went to bed at eleven and had been lying there ever since, staring at his ceiling. He reached over and grabbed his phone on the nightstand. He looked at the photo one more time. The blood looked real enough. And the pose Sharon was in looked like something someone might fall into after being shot, but ultimately, he knew it was all fake. The man on the phone had been telling the truth. Tate was playing him.

Anger and frustration coursed through him. Tomorrow morning, he would have to hit the safe deposit box and take out a hundred thousand dollars. That was his money, his and Sharon's. They had been saving it to buy a beach house in the Keys. That was a plan from a different lifetime. Truthfully, it was probably divorce money, half a million dollars of it. That, along with the house and cars, was what he would have had to pay her to make the divorce as quick and easy as possible. She had no job, so Richard wouldn't be entitled to any alimony. He would lose his job at the firm. In exchange, he would get custody of Eliza—and not a dime to take care of her.

The past few hours had brought nothing but anguish, but he decided he'd done the only thing he could have. He'd made the only decision that made sense. He wouldn't live a life in a studio apartment with a daughter who would end up hating him. Getting rid of Sharon was the only way. He just wished he'd taken more time to select the people to do it.

He sat up on the edge of the bed, his face in his hands, and exhaled. Sleep wasn't going to come. He went back down to the movie room and turned on a movie. He stared blankly at the screen, not following or listening to what was going on. His guts were a rumbling mess of nerves.

33

Stanton slept on a couch in the precinct's break room. From one until five in the morning, he was alone. But at five, during the patrol shift change, people started coming in for coffee. Each one made noise that woke him. He turned into the cushions and hoped they would dampen the sound, but they didn't. By six, he figured he'd let Sticks stew long enough. Stanton guessed Sticks was high on meth, maybe even PCP, when he'd brought him in. The withdrawals would get worse as the hours ticked away and the high wore off. The worse Sticks felt, the more his body would turn against him, and the more supple he would be during their discussion.

Stanton retrieved his gun and badge from his locker then stumbled to the bathroom and splashed cold water on his face. He stared at himself in the mirror. Everyone always told him he appeared much younger than his years, and he could see it. Other than the dark circles that had been a permanent fixture over the past few years, he looked no more than twenty-nine or thirty.

Stanton walked slowly down the corridor toward Interrogation Five. He peered through the glass and saw Sticks huddled against the wall, shivering and sweating. His shirt was soaked. Methamphetamine withdrawals started quick, but not that quick. Sticks was addicted to PCP, the most dangerous drug on the street. That meant he was unpredictable, possibly even psychotic. Stanton didn't want his firearm in there with a crazy man, so he walked back to his locker and secured it before heading back to the interrogation room.

He shut the door behind him and sat at the table, then he waited until Sticks spoke first.

"Don't—don't you want to talk to me?"

"Are you ready to talk?" Stanton asked.

"I ain't feelin' too good, man. May need a hospital."

"They won't give you any drugs. They'll pick up on your PCP addiction as fast as I did. They'll want you to detox before they do anything."

He put his head down, rocking slightly back and forth. "Ain't that a bitch," he said, through chattering teeth.

"Tell me about Tate."

"What about him?"

"Why did he kill that boy?"

Sticks glanced up at him then back down. "What boy?"

Stanton rose. "I'm not playing games. I can hold you for seventy-two hours without charging you, and this is where you're going to be while I go arrest your uncle."

Stanton turned to leave, and Sticks shouted, "Wait. Wait, man. Sit down. Sit down."

He sat.

"I didn't see it. I was comin' outta the house when he shot that kid."

"What were you doing at the house?"

Sticks swore under his breath. "I want some fuckin'—what'dya call it? Where I don't get this shit on me."

"You want immunity. Tell me what you know, and we'll talk to the prosecutor."

He chewed his lip. "We was there for the wife. Fuckin' what's her name? Sharon. We was supposed to kill her, and then this girl was there in the house, and I guess Hiapo grabbed her."

"Hiapo who?"

"I don't know his last name. Friend of Tate's. They met in the can."

"Why were you there for Sharon?"

"Her husband paid us to kill her. A hundred Gs, man. You believe that shit? A hundred Gs for one bullet."

Stanton's guts were tight with anger. He felt it rising in his throat and had to push it back down. "Richard Miller hired you to kill his wife? You heard him say that?"

"Nah, man. He set it all up with Tate. I didn't do shit. I ran into the house and grabbed some jewelry outta her room. That was it. That's all I done."

Stanton was quiet for a moment. "Where is Tate?"

"He in an RV. With some dude named Lee."

"Lee what?"

"I dunno his last name. But I got his number in my phone. But y'all took my phone away."

"I'll find it. Is there anything else I should know?"

"That ain't enough?"

Stanton rose and stood over Sticks. He bent down to look him in the eyes. "If you're lying to me, I'll make sure your uncle knows you sold him out." He turned and left the interrogation room.



Sticks's phone had been held for transport to the evidence locker as part of the potential kidnapping of Sharon and Eliza Miller. Stanton showed his police department ID to the evidence clerk, and she opened the door for him.

The evidence was arranged by date and case number. A small box contained Sticks's phone. Wearing latex gloves, Stanton took it out and turned it on. He found Lee's contact information. No last name. Stanton dialed from his own cell to avoid Sticks's name appearing on the ID.

"Yo," a young man's voice answered.

"Yes," Stanton said in the best upbeat, innocent voice he could muster, "I'm looking for Lee?"

"Who dis?"

"Well, it's a private matter concerning a possible false checking account being opened in your name. I'm just calling to verify if you've opened an account recently. Oh, I guess we should verify your information first. Sorry. I have you as Lee Roberts. Is that correct?"

"Nah, man. It's Lee Philips. What about a checking account?"

"Philips, hm… you may not be the Lee I need. Are you over there at 1597 Coconut Parrish?"

"No, that ain't me."

"What was your address?"

"I'm up on Ashgrove."

"Ashgrove. Yeah, that's definitely not you. Just a mix-up with the names in the computer, I bet. I'm sorry to have wasted your time."

"A'ight."

Stanton turned off Sticks's phone, placed it back in the evidence bag, and headed for his Jeep.

34

In the morning, Richard woke up after what must've been no more than two hours of sleep. He felt dizzy and weak, as if he'd been drinking all night or had the flu. In the bathroom, he kept urinating outside the bowl and thought about wiping it up with toilet paper. But it was Saturday; the maids would be coming that day. *Let them clean it up.*

He hopped into the shower and nearly fell asleep with his head leaned against the wall. He forced himself awake then slapped his face a couple of times.

After his shower, he went downstairs to have breakfast by himself and think. All he had to do was think everything through. But without sleep, he didn't believe he was doing very well at it. He decided to pick up some Ambien from his doctor.

On his way to the kitchen, he saw something outside the living room windows—flashing lights. He walked up to the windows and looked out. Several police cruisers were barreling toward his house. One slammed on its brakes in front, and three officers jumped out.

"Shit!" Richard sprinted to the back of the house. He had a gun and cash upstairs but no time to get them. He could get the money from the safe deposit box anyway. He was almost to the back door when he realized he needed his keys and ID to get into the safe deposit box. He ran back to the kitchen and grabbed them just as someone pounded on his front door.

He ran out to the back. His backyard was encircled by a high fence with only one locked gate, and no officers had made their way over it yet. Richard raced across the yard and jumped over the fence, falling onto his face into his neighbor's yard.

He dashed across the yard and into another neighbor's yard then went in the opposite direction of his house. Running on the pavement, he felt pain in his feet and realized he wasn't wearing any shoes.

*Never heard any sirens. In the movies, they always turned their sirens on.*

The street he was on wound up a hill then came out near an upscale country club, where he could buy shoes in the pro shop.

He took out his membership ID as he went inside. He rode the elevator to the bottom floor, where he had to scan his ID to get to the store. It was packed with swimsuits and gym clothing. Richard bought socks and sneakers. The cashier glanced at his shoeless feet but didn't say anything.

"Lost my shoes," he said awkwardly.

He decided the club gym was a good place to hide out for a couple of hours. The police would be at his home and work. But they wouldn't guess he belonged to the club. Not right away anyhow.

Richard walked out to the pool area and collapsed into a deck chair. His heart felt as though it were pounding so hard it might stop. He went to check the time on his phone and realized he didn't have it.

"Shit."

His mind began churning, spitting out ideas. He could live in the jungle or buy a little cabin somewhere. No, they would find him. Leaving the island—maybe even the country—was the best thing. He'd been to Canada several times and enjoyed it. He liked England. His only problem was getting the money to go. He had over half a million in his safe deposit box, but did the police know about that already? No way—how could they? Only he and Sharon knew about it, and she was gone. Unless the cops already had her.

"Shit, shit, shit."

He stood, and marched out of the pool area. Then he bought a wide-brim hat and sunglasses on the way out of the club. He needed to get to the bank right as it opened.

35

The basement walls pushed in on him. Tate paced between them, the gun in his hand. He heard a voice, and only after a few minutes did he realize he'd been talking to himself. He had urinated in his pants, and the warmth had long ago turned to coolness down his leg, but he didn't care. None of that mattered.

His mind was a blur of images and thoughts. He thought briefly that it would be fun to stab himself through the tongue with the coat hanger lying in Lee's basement. That was when he grasped that he'd smoked too much angel dust. The shit was in his system, permeating his mind. He kept smoking weed to calm himself, but it wasn't working.

Lee came down the stairs, and their eyes locked.

"Yo, you don't look so good, man. You a'ight?"

"No," Tate said, continuing to pace. "Shit's fucked up. Shit's fucked up today."

"Smoke a bowl and calm down."

"I have been smoking bowls," Tate growled.

"Easy, bra. Easy. You want somethin' to eat?"

"Yeah, yeah. Yeah, get me… get me a hamburger and curly fries and chicken, and—and fuckin' sandwiches. Meatball sandwiches. And chips."

"Okay, man. You just chill, a'ight. I'll see what I can get."

As Lee headed upstairs, he heard Tate talking to himself. That wasn't good. Tate was unstable enough as it was. Lee jogged up the stairs and out to the RV. Hiapo was asleep, as was the young girl. The woman was sitting on the toilet, her hands still bound with duct tape.

Lee was about to wake Hiapo when the woman said, "I have to use the bathroom."

Lee looked up at her. "What?"

"I said, I have to use the bathroom."

"I don't give a shit."

"Unless you want a mess in here, I need to use the bathroom."

Lee exhaled. Hiapo was sound asleep, snoring in fact. Lee kicked him, but the big man didn't even stir. "Fine."

Lee walked to the back of the RV. He helped the woman up off the toilet. As he bent down to flip open the toilet seat, he felt an impact like a brick against his head and his forehead slammed into the toilet. He bounced off and lay on his back on the floor. The woman had something in her hands—a small black box, like a TV or DVD player.

The woman sprinted off the RV, leaving Lee cussing and grabbing the back of his head. He could feel the blood seeping over his fingers.

He jumped up. "Fucking bitch!"

Lee dashed after the woman. Screaming, she ran up the sidewalk, and Lee followed. A loud pop echoed through the neighborhood, and the woman collapsed. Lee instinctively hit the ground. His eyes darted around until he saw Tate standing on the front lawn, a gun in his hand.

He walked up to the woman and fired three more rounds. Lee covered his ears with trembling fingers. Tate yelled at the corpse.

He ran up to Lee and shouted, "Fuck you!" Then he pointed the weapon at Lee's head.

"Nah, Tate, man. Nah, I ain't done nothin'. Tate!"

Lee didn't hear a pop or any more shouting. There was only a slight pain in his head then darkness.

36

The police cruisers just ahead of them slammed on their brakes in front of the home. Stanton jumped out of the car as soon as Laka pulled their car to a stop. The Kevlar vest made Stanton feel heavy and immobile, but he knew how necessary it was.

A SWAT van pulled up just then. The SWAT commander was heading the operation. As Stanton walked over to him to confirm the strike, he saw the body on the sidewalk—a black male with a head wound. Just ahead of him was a woman whose wrists were bound with duct tape.

Stanton ran to the bodies. The man was cold and had been dead for hours. The woman was even colder, and most of her blood had pooled around her. Stanton recognized Sharon Miller from a photo of her in Richard Miller's house.

He scanned the street for an RV, but there wasn't one.

"What the hell happened?" Laka asked, jogging up to him.

"The way she fell, it looks like she was running when the round entered the back of her head. But him—I don't know why he was shot."

"Maybe he was gonna sell him out?"

"Maybe. Let's hang back and let SWAT do their job."

The SWAT team was a precision instrument. They didn't have a wide range of functions within the police department, but the ones they did have, they executed better than anyone. After a shout, they knocked down the front door and delivered the tear gas. Then they slammed through the side and backdoors nearly in unison. The men shouted constantly as they cleared one room then another. Smoke billowed out from the living room window then swirled in the breeze before disappearing.

The SWAT commander came out a few minutes later. He lifted his mask and stood in front of Stanton with his rifle slung over his shoulder.

"House is clear, Detective."

"You sure?" Stanton knew he was and that he'd probably checked everything several times, but he couldn't think of anything else to say. The frustration of having Tate slip through his fingers was too much.

"Positive."

"Thanks."

Stanton watched the house. The forensics techs had arrived and were analyzing the bodies. A few of them were staring at the SWAT members in wonder and awe. The two groups worked in the same factory but couldn't have been more different.

"Don't worry," Laka said, "We'll get him."

Stanton shook his head. "Before he kills the girl?"

Laka didn't respond. Stanton strode into the house. The tear gas had cleared, and a few SWAT team members were mulling around the living room. They filed out of the house when they saw him. A couple uniforms were around, surveying the scene for their supplemental reports.

Stanton sat down on the sofa. The living room had only two windows, and both were blacked out with what looked like black paint or tar. He could only see because of the light coming in from the open door. He put his hands on his thighs and stared at the carpet. Sharon Miller was dead. He hadn't gotten to her in time. All that work, all that effort, and she had died. And her daughter would probably soon follow. And to top it off, he had just gotten word that Richard Miller was MIA.

"You all right?" Laka asked, sitting down in the recliner across from him.

"No, I don't think so."

"What's wrong?"

"The girl. I just keep thinking if I'd have worked a little faster... I don't know. I don't know."

"This isn't anything you did, Jon. Her dickhead father put evil out there, and that's what this poor family saw the universe give back to them. The father started this, not you."

"I couldn't save her," he mumbled, more to himself than anyone else. "I did everything I could, and it wasn't enough."

"Sometimes it isn't. But you just pick up and keep going. We'll find her. You have to believe that."

Stanton leaned back on the sofa and looked around the living room. Everything was old and weathered except the television, which was at least eighty inches and clean enough to be brand-new.

An island-wide BOLO—be on the look-out—call had been sent out for any RVs matching the description Sticks had given him. Stanton could think of nothing else to do but wait.

"Tate's gonna wanna get off the island," Laka said. "He might need somebody to help him with that."

Stanton thought for a moment. "The only person on the island that would possibly help him is his wife." He bit the inside of his cheek and ran his tongue over the membrane—a habit he'd had since he was a child. "Better than sitting around eating bagels. Let's go pay her another visit."

37

In the noonday heat, Richard dripped sweat. He decided he needed new clothes before anything else. But he was scared the police could follow his credit card transactions. But, then again, by the time the police saw his credit card history for today, he would be long gone. They already knew he was still on the island, so he wouldn't really be giving anything away if he just ran in and bought shorts, a nice button-down shirt, and sandals. He decided it was worth the risk. His suit was too hot, and the pressure of his tie around his neck felt like a noose. It'd never felt that way before.

A strip mall wasn't far from where he was. He tipped his hat low as he walked down the street. It was a woman's hat, and he wondered if it was actually drawing more attention to him. He tossed it in the bushes on the walk to the mall.

The sidewalks were never really very swamped in downtown Honolulu, considering how large the city really was. A lot of people from the mainland moved there, thinking it would be paradise, only to find the cost of living was double or triple of where they had come from.

The strip mall was just across the street from where he was, and he considered jaywalking, but instead, he walked the extra hundred feet to the crosswalk at the intersection. He glanced into each car as he crossed, wondering if someone would recognize him. He didn't know if his face was on TV.

The mall had at least twenty stores. When he spotted the Polo store, he practically ran in. Then he forced himself to take his time perusing the shorts. He found a pair he liked then chose a polo shirt and sandals. After he purchased them, he asked the cashier if he could use the changing room, then someone else on the floor unlocked one for him. He hung up his suit and looked at it one more time. Leaving it was such a shame. *The price of freedom,* he guessed.

As he headed out of the store, he stopped at the cashier's counter. "Um, sorry, is there someplace here that sells phones?"

"Yeah," the cashier said, not taking his eyes off the shirt he was folding. "Just up is a Sprint or something."

"Thanks."

Richard marched over there. The two men behind the desk were talking and laughing.

"Hi," he said. "I was wondering if you guys had any disposable phones?"

"Not here, no. There's a Safeway right up the street, and they got some."

"Thanks a bunch."

The Safeway was another short walk, and getting around in his sandals felt better than his walking in his wingtips. Pleasant music was playing inside the store as he entered, and Richard hummed along. Given everything that had happened, he had to admit that he wasn't in a particularly bad mood.

Richard found the phones right at the front of one of the aisles. After purchasing a phone and minutes card, he went out to the curb and set them up. Once the phone was activated, he called the only person he could think to call: his lawyer.

"Strain, Klep and Barnum," the receptionist said.

"Yeah, hi. Can I speak to Candace Strain, please?"

"May I ask who's calling?"

"Um, is this Marleen?"

"Yes."

"Oh, hi. It's Richard."

Silence.

"Um, Richard Miller. I work there."

"Oh, right, Richard. Sorry. Yeah, Candace is here. Hold on a sec, 'kay?"

"Okay."

The line clicked, and Candace's voice came on. "Richard, what can I do for you?"

That was a good sign. The police were probably staked out outside the offices, but word hadn't yet reached Candace.

"Um, Candace, I think I'm going to need you to be my lawyer. You're the best lawyer I know, so I thought I would call you."

"Your lawyer for what?"

"I've done some questionable things, Candace." Richard swallowed. He couldn't believe he was sitting on the curb, begging his boss to represent him.

"How questionable?"

"Well, I may have set some things in motion, and people got hurt. I don't know that for sure, but I think maybe. I may have hired someone to hurt my wife."

A long silence.

"Um, Candace? You there?"

"I'm here. Is Sharon dead, Richard?"

"I don't know. I can't contact the people I hired anymore."

"You need to turn yourself in."

A car passed, and Richard glanced up at the driver then let his eyes drift back to the pavement. "I don't think that's a good idea. I need you to help me get off the island."

"That's not what criminal lawyers do. I'll represent you, Richard. But the only way for me to do that is if you turn yourself in. I'll be there with you to make sure they don't ask any questions. But the process can't even start until you turn yourself in."

"I... well, I'll get back to you on that."

"What the hell happened, Richard?"

"It's a long story, I guess. I'll call you later, okay?"

"Okay. If you do get arrested, don't say anything to the police. Just give them my name and number."

"Will do."

Richard hung up. Speaking to her had actually made him feel better. He liked knowing someone out there was on his side. But she was completely wrong. There was no point in turning himself in. Hawaii didn't have the death penalty, but he would be an old man before he got out of prison. He wasn't about to let that happen.

So that left one problem: how to get off the island. There wasn't a chance that the police hadn't notified all the airports. But cruises left from Oahu all the time. Maybe the authorities hadn't notified all the cruise lines yet?

He rose, brushed off his bottom, and began walking.

38

Hiapo sat at the table as the RV raced down the freeway. He glanced back at the girl, who was huddled on the bed, crying. He'd woken to gunshots and discovered that the woman was gone. He didn't need to ask what had happened.

Tate was driving—and mumbling to himself. Hiapo had never seen him like that before. He rose from the table and sat in the passenger seat. Tate's face looked different. It was pale and glistening with sweat.

"You good?" Hiapo asked.

"No, man. I'm pretty fucking far from good."

"What's wrong?"

"Everything. Shit's just fucked up today, man."

Hiapo sat quietly for a second, then glanced back at the crying girl. "Maybe we should pull over somewhere so you can sleep."

"I don't need to sleep."

"You been smokin' that shit, ain't you?"

Tate looked at him with wide eyes, full of fear. "What the fuck did you say?"

"You need to chill, bra. We need to pull over and get something for you to sleep."

"Fuck you. Fuck you!" He pulled out his pistol and pressed the muzzle against Hiapo's head. "Get your ass back there and shut your fucking mouth!"

Hiapo didn't flinch. That wasn't the first time he'd had a gun against his head. But Tate wasn't himself. Hiapo looked at him and didn't recognize the man looking back.

Hiapo rose without a word and went back to the table. He looked at the girl then at Tate. He was talking to himself again, and he laughed. Hiapo shook his head and sat back down.

After nearly an hour of riding, Hiapo knew where they were going—a cabin. It was really just a shack that Tate's father had owned. His father had lived in the jungle, away from everyone else. He owned his cabin, a few clothes, his guns, and that was it. He lived off the land. Tate had said he'd snapped later in life.

After the family moved from California, Tate's father had stayed with them for only a short while before disappearing into the jungle. Tate saw him regularly, and his father had taught him how to fish and how to shoot. He and Hiapo had stayed there several times when they had to let shit cool down.

As the RV traveled the dirt road leading up a hill, trees surrounded it. Hiapo watched the jungle as they drove. Other cabins were there, too. The area wasn't as secluded as he'd remembered it. The RV eventually came to a stop in front of a brown cabin with only two windows. The gun still in his hand, Tate got out of the RV without a word and went inside the cabin.

39

Stanton brought the car to a stop, and Laka was the first to get out. Stanton stared at the home for a while. A wave of pity for Cindy Reynolds washed over him. As he got out of the car, she peeked through the blinds in the front room.

Laka knocked, but the door didn't open.

Stanton shouted, "Cindy, please open up. I saw you look through the blinds. I don't want to have to get a warrant."

A moment later, the lock turned, and she peered out over a chain on the door.

"May we come in?" Stanton asked.

She nodded then shut the door, unlatched the chain, and let them in.

The house was cluttered, and a cat, which Stanton hadn't seen last time he was there, occupied the couch. He sat near it, and the cat wandered over to lie on his lap. Animals had always liked him. He rubbed the cat behind its ear for a few moments before speaking. Laka chose to stand with her arms folded, her eyes locked onto Cindy, who sat nervously across from Stanton.

"We need to know where he is, Cindy. And I know you know."

"I don't."

"He's killed three people. One of them was an eleven-year-old boy. He has a thirteen-year-old girl with him now. I need to save her life, Cindy. And you're the only one that can help me."

She swallowed, rubbing her hands together. "I…"

"He's done this before. Left you by yourself to deal with his messes. I know you love him. I'm not questioning your love for him. But I know you're not like him. You care about people. I can see it in your eyes. You don't want this girl to die because we couldn't get to her in time. You don't want to live with that. Tell me where I can find him, and I promise you I'll do everything in my power to protect him. I'm not promising he'll walk away from this without consequences, but I won't let anyone hurt him."

Her hands trembled as she spoke. "We had a daughter once. Gloria. Our little girl."

"What happened to her?"

"She was taken away from us. 'Cause of the drugs. She lives in San Francisco now, with a nice family. But the family don't let us see her. They think it's bad for her to see her own parents. But I can see why. We ain't no good for her."

"I'm sorry, Cindy. I'm sorry that this is where Tate brought you. But I need your help. I want that girl to have a chance at life. Just like your own daughter has now."

She nodded. "He has a cabin his father left him…"

40

Hiapo watched as Tate paced back and forth in front of the cabin. His hands were shaking so badly that the gun slipped and fell on the ground several times. Hiapo stood next to the girl right outside the RV.

Tate was mumbling to himself and kicking bits of dirt. He placed the gun against his head and closed his eyes. Then he started ranting again.

"I'm better than you," Tate shouted. "I'm fuckin'… I'm better. I was there, man. I was fucking there."

Hiapo didn't move. He kept his eyes on Tate, his brow furrowed. The big man glanced at the girl, who was trembling. A stream of urine ran down her leg. Hiapo had a weapon, too. He casually reached his hand back and felt the grip of the pistol. That would be a last resort.

He didn't understand why white folks messed with something that could screw up their entire mind. His people, from his ancestors down to his father, preferred the more subtle drugs. Awa, a type of kava root, and marijuana were the favored ones. Those drugs gave the user an appreciation of things around them, connected them to nature, and made them happy to live in the most beautiful place on the planet. Why anyone would want to take a drug that made them cut themselves and jump off buildings, he couldn't understand.

"Fucking fuck!" Tate screamed. He was hunched over, his hands on his head.

"Tate," Hiapo said calmly, "you need to go to a hospital."

He instantly straightened, holding the weapon tightly in his shaky hands. He raised it and pointed it at Hiapo's face.

"That's what you think, huh? You think I'm stupid. You want me to go there 'cause that's where they gonna be waitin' for me."

"I want you there 'cause I'm your friend, bra."

"My friend? You ain't my friend. I know who you work for. I know what you want!"

Hiapo looked down to the girl. "Run," he told her.

She didn't wait for him to say it again. She looked from him to Tate then turned and sprinted for the surrounding jungle. Tate's weapon moved toward her.

"You ain't gonna be shootin' her," Hiapo said, pulling out his pistol.

Tate jerked. The two men had their pistols trained on each other. Hiapo was calm, his hand steady. Sweat was pouring into Tate's eyes, and he was moving around. Over the past hour, his tremors had gotten worse. Hiapo didn't think he could have hit a car that was right in front of him in his condition.

"Put the piece down, bra."

"Fuck you!" he shouted. "You want me to go in. You want me to live in a cage again."

"Ain't no one gonna turn you in. But I'm leaving, bra. You can stay here in the jungle."

"You ain't goin' nowhere."

Hiapo lowered the pistol slightly, aiming for Tate's heart. He'd never been a good shot, and he needed a bigger target.

"We brothers, T. We did time together, man."

"And you're throwin' it out like it didn't mean nothin'.'"

"Nobody's called the cops, man. It's that shit you been smokin'. It's messing with your head. Your mind, man, it's playin' tricks on you, T."

"It was—it was you. You put that shit in me—in my drink. In my drinks I was drinking this morning, and you put that shit in 'em."

There was no talking to him. He was gone. Hiapo decided the only thing he could do was leave. He started backing up toward the RV then thought better of it. The cops were probably looking for it already. Lee's neighbors had definitely called them after hearing the gunshots. Better to walk.

Hiapo, his weapon still held on Tate, began to circle him, heading for the dirt road back to the freeway. He could hitch a ride there, call a cab, or something.

"You ain't leavin'," Tate said.

"Don't do it, bra."

"You ain't leavin' this place alive."

Hiapo's chest felt tight. He was tough—he had faced countless fistfights, and he'd even been shot before. But a sick feeling in his gut told him he might not make it out of there. He stopped walking and wrapped both hands around the pistol. Better to take him out right away.

Tate sprang forward. Hiapo only got off one shot before Tate closed the distance between them. The shot missed, leaving Tate only a few feet away. He fired back. All three rounds connected. Tate had held the pistol low, so two rounds went into Hiapo's hip, and one went into his thigh. Hiapo's gun dropped out of his hand as he collapsed into the dirt with a groan.

"Told you you ain't leavin' alive."

Tate lifted the weapon then stopped. He looked back to where the girl had run into the jungle then walked that way. Without looking at Hiapo, he fired another two rounds. One slammed into Hiapo's chest. He heard a sucking sound and saw the blood pouring out of him as Tate ran into the jungle after the girl.

41

The police cruiser raced up the dirt road, with Stanton bouncing around in the passenger seat. Laka was in the backseat, and a uniform was driving. Stanton watched the surrounding jungles. He'd never been to the jungle area before, and the lush vegetation was something else. Reds, greens, and yellows. Massive trees hung over everything like watchful guardians, their arms dangling dangerously close to the road.

The three cruisers behind them had their lights on but no sirens. Stanton caught a glimpse of the two officers in the car directly behind his. They were laughing as they flew over a bump, the car's tires leaving the ground. They were enjoying the chase.

A long time ago, when he'd been a different person, he had enjoyed the chase, too. Every small step toward his prey sent a rush of adrenaline through him. The thrill of the hunt was so intense sometimes that it kept him up and working all night. He'd lived for the job. And what he got in return was a failed marriage, two kids whose childhoods he'd missed, and a fiancée who'd left him before the wedding. He'd given everything to the job and gotten nothing in return.

The chase meant little to him anymore. He didn't hunt for the thrill of catching the prey. There was something more primal involved. He called it justice in his own thoughts, but he knew that wasn't what it was. It was revenge—pure, cold revenge. Adam Cummings couldn't avenge his death. Sharon Miller couldn't avenge hers. They were counting on him. But vengeance brought no pleasure. It never had.

The GPS dinged, announcing that they had arrived at the location Cindy had described. About two hundred feet ahead was the cabin she had told Stanton about. In front of it was an RV.

Stanton was the first one out of the cruiser. He withdrew his Desert Eagle from its holster and kept it low as he trotted over and poked his head into the RV. Convinced no one was inside, he took the steps up just to make sure Eliza wasn't bound and gagged in the back.

The RV stank like sweat, body odor, and burning plastic. He knew the smell. PCP. The drug had a unique scent that no other drug could match. It was an absolutely artificial stench. Nothing in nature smelled that way.

Laka came up behind him, her gun drawn. She inhaled, and her nose crinkled like a bulldog's.

"PCP. I know that smell anywhere," she said. "You're right. If anything would make him snap, it's that. I once saw a guy start biting the police cruiser after we arrested him because he was high on the stuff. Broke every tooth in his mouth, but he didn't stop."

Stanton didn't respond. His eyes were scanning the trash on the floor. Burnt roaches, empty beer cans, and containers of food… No blood.

Stanton looked out the windshield and saw the officers carrying a battering ram surrounding the cabin. "Police search warrant!" one man yelled before the team smashed the ram into the door near the doorknob.

It flew open, and officers swarmed in. Stanton ran out and slowly looked over the property. Small footprints, about the size of a teenager's, marked the dirt, leading up a path to a grove of trees. They were mixed with larger prints.

"You coming?" Laka said, heading to the cabin.

"They're not in there."

Stanton noticed a body lying near the RV. Hiapo, he guessed. The man's eyes were glazed over with death, a look he knew well. Ignoring the body, Stanton dashed into the trees.


The path was relatively clear despite the dense surrounding jungles. As he ran, he came across a trail. He looked one way then the other. The trail had so many prints that he couldn't distinguish the ones he'd been following anymore.

One path, the one to the left, seemed to go deeper into the jungle. The other headed back toward the freeway. He guessed she'd gone right. He pumped his legs, holstering his weapon so he could jog at a quicker pace without worrying about the gun in his hand. The trail looped around and up a hill. He could hear a waterfall nearby. As he passed the waterfall, a much quieter sound caught his attention. With the pounding water right next to him, he couldn't tell what the noise was. Just in case, he withdrew his weapon and darted past the waterfall.

He heard the sound again, and it made him stop. He was breathing deeply but not heavily. He calmed his breath to hear better. The sound was coming from off the trail, somewhere east of him. He headed into the vegetation.

Outside of the cities, Oahu was nearly feral. Stanton knew that some of the jungle plants were poisonous to the touch, but he hadn't been in Hawaii long enough to know which ones. He'd heard from others in the force that some of the plants could make people itch, and some could cause illness. But he had no choice. He heard the sound again and knew he was going in the right direction.

He came to a clearing and saw movement off to the side. A young girl was on the ground, and a white man in jeans was growling something at her.

Stanton tried to be as quiet as possible, but he had to scrape past several bushes to get out into the clearing. The man heard. He grabbed the girl by the hair and lifted her to her knees. He stood behind her and placed his gun against her head.

"Let her go, Tate."

"Fuck you. Fuck you! I'll fucking kill her. Don't come closer. I'll kill her!"

"I believe you," Stanton said, holding up his hands, letting his weapon dangle from his thumb. "I believe you. I'll put my gun down if you put yours down."

"Yeah… yeah, that's what you want. That's what you say. That's what you say!"

"Let her go, Tate. If you want a hostage, I'm a much better one than her. Take me and let her go."

Tate twitched. His eyes closed, and he shook his head, tremors quivering through his body from his shoulders down to his legs. Stanton had never seen something like that before. Tate Reynolds didn't seem to be there anymore. There would be no negotiation. He lowered his hands. He had promised Cindy that he would do everything he could to protect Tate. But Eliza had to come first. He had no choice in the matter.

"Fine, I'm leaving," Stanton said.

"You go. You go!"

Stanton turned around. He had one shot, maybe two. His heart was pounding in his ears. He felt the weight of the gun and the sweat rolling down his forehead. He closed his eyes and said a prayer.

In an instant, Stanton spun around. Tate's eyes went wide, and he tried to lift the gun and fire. Stanton fired first. The first round missed, but the second hit Tate's shoulder. As if the bullet had hit a soft melon, blood spattered to the sides, and a thump echoed off the trees. Most of Tate's left shoulder was gone, but he didn't fall back. He actually sprinted at Stanton.

Stanton held the gun firmly, hoping he wouldn't have to fire again, but Tate didn't stop.

"I don't want to kill you. Stop, please!"

Tate was screaming like a warrior running into battle. The consciousness reflected in his eyes, the part of him that told others there was a reasoning person in there, was gone. Nothing was left.

Stanton put two rounds in the man's chest, knocking him off his feet and onto his back. Even on the ground Tate continued to writhe and spit. He still had the gun in his hand, so Stanton couldn't approach the girl without risking getting shot himself. But he wouldn't fire on a man who was already down.

Instead, Stanton waited a few moments. As the blood poured out of Tate Reynolds, his movements grew slow and weak. And eventually, he lay still.

Slowly, Stanton walked to him and placed his foot over Tate's wrist. He knelt, took the gun, and tossed it aside. Tate's eyes were wide and rimmed with a deep red. Hemorrhaging had occurred inside his eyes. Stanton bent down and placed his fingers on Tate's neck. There was no pulse. He holstered his weapon and rose to check on the girl.

42

The cabin was swarming with forensic techs and investigators looking for evidence of other crimes, but Stanton knew they wouldn't find anything. They thought maybe Tate had made a habit of bringing people to the cabin to kill them, but Stanton didn't think so. This kidnapping was an isolated incident.

Stanton handed over his gun and badge to the two Internal Affairs detectives who had shown up. Any time an officer was involved in a shooting, Internal Affairs Division made an appearance. Stanton had found that no matter the police agency, it took a special type of person to investigate and arrest his or her own co-workers.

The detectives took a quick statement from him then asked that he come in for a formal interview the following day. They informed Stanton that he was officially on paid leave until he was cleared of the shooting.

When he was through with IAD, he watched the two bodies being hauled away. Laka told him that as soon as he ran off into the jungle, an officer had spotted the body of Tate's accomplice, the one Stanton had already seen. The paramedics told Stanton that one of the slugs had nicked his femoral artery in his thigh—a one in a hundred shot. The man had bled out and died within five minutes of being shot.

Stanton walked over to the ambulance where Eliza Miller was sitting in the back, getting evaluated. She had no injuries, but they were worried about shock. Stanton could sense that she was much stronger than she let on. She would be fine, eventually.

"You doing okay?" he asked.

She nodded but didn't say anything.

"They're going to take you to the hospital, Eliza. I'll come by and visit to make sure you're okay. Do you want me to bring anything when I come by? Any special clothes from your house or something to eat?"

She shook her head. "Where's my mom?"

Stanton had to look away at the men going in and out of the cabin. He didn't speak for so long that she understood, and she began to sob. When he put his arm around her, she didn't push him away. They sat that way for a long time until the paramedics finally told him they had to leave. Stanton let her go and watched as the ambulance drove away. Her father had probably fled the state. She was an orphan, for all intents and purposes. And why? Because her father didn't have the courage to face her mother and tell her their marriage was over. Instead, he'd put evil into the world, and it had engulfed everything in his life.

"Do you wanna stay a little longer?" Laka asked as she came up next to him.

"No. I've had enough of this place."

43

The office was cooler than it normally was. Stanton could hear an air conditioner running somewhere as he waited. A new painting was hanging in Dr. Vaquer's lobby, or maybe it was an old painting that he hadn't noticed before. Stanton knew the painting. It was a recreation of Rothko's *Pretty Color Palette*. The whites and blues melded into something unique that brought emotion to the surface without words. Stanton got the sensation of staring into a tunnel or maybe falling.

Dr. Vaquer opened the doors and welcomed him back. He rose and followed her inside. The couch felt softer somehow.

"So," she said, "how are you doing?"

"I was put back on duty two days ago and cleared for the shooting."

"That's good news for you, I assume."

"Why do you assume?"

She grinned slightly. "Don't be coy, Jon. You know how I feel about you in police work."

"Yeah, I know."

"So how do you feel now that the case is over?"

"I don't know. I guess like a heavy weight was taken off my chest. It felt like it was getting harder and harder to breathe as the case went on, and then suddenly, that feeling was gone, and everything went back to normal."

"Until the next one, you mean."

"I guess."

"I read a little about the case in the *Oahu Sun*. They said that the husband was never caught. Is that true?"

"Yes. He cleared out their safe deposit box. We found a ticket a few days after the shooting for a cruise ship headed to Baja. We put in a BOLO request with the sheriff's offices down there, but I doubt they care much about that. A lot of people go to Mexico to get lost."

She nodded. "How does that make you feel? That the man who put everything in motion has gotten away with it?"

"I don't know that he has."

"Why do you say that?"

"It's like you told me once. Whatever you put out there is what you get back. I think I believe that."

"Evil people prosper all the time. CEOs, politicians, billionaires… there are a lot of successful people that rose to where they are because of their lack of empathy."

"I know, but I don't believe they're happy. I can't believe that. I think it'd be hard for me to do what I do if I didn't believe in some sort of justice. That's why Richard Miller's escape doesn't bother me as much as I think it should."

"We've talked about this before, this belief in retribution. Do you believe that applies to you, as well?"

"Of course. I've done terrible things. I neglected my wife and children. I killed people. I've lied to get confessions… I've done a lot. And I don't know what's waiting for me, but I know it's something. I can't get away with all that forever."

"Well, maybe losing your wife and kids is the punishment. Maybe the anguish and the sleepless nights and the depression are the retribution, and there's no grim ending out there?"

"Maybe. I don't know." He exhaled loudly. "I was hoping we could cut today's session a little short."

"Certainly. May I ask why?"

"I've got a date."

She grinned. "Really? That's fantastic. With whom?"

"Her name's Debbie. I've ditched her a couple of times. I was making the same mistake I made with Melissa and Emma. Good women I left behind for the job. I don't want to do that to her."

"Well, I think that is about the best thing you've told me in here."

He nodded. "I wanted to talk about something first, though."

"What?"

"We've never talked at length about the disappearance of my sister. It's not something I talk to a lot of people about."

"I understand."

"I think I've told you that she disappeared from a movie theater when she was out with her friends in Seattle. The police didn't really turn anything up. I tried investigating it myself, but I was a kid. I didn't know anything." He paused. "I'm giving serious thought to taking a leave of absence from the Honolulu PD and going to Seattle."

She watched him for a moment. "Are you telling me you're thinking about investigating the disappearance of your sister?"

"Yes. I want to know what you think about it?"

"I think we don't always want to know the truth. I think the truth can be more painful than the not knowing."

"You wouldn't say that if it was your sister."

"You didn't let me finish. I also think that closure really is the first step in the healing process. You were admitted to medical school but chose not to go. You have a doctorate in psychology and had a reputation as a good professor. And even though you admittedly enjoyed both careers more than police work, you stayed with the police force because you considered yourself mediocre in those other fields. Those things speak about the power that unresolved issue has over your past."

"You think I'm a cop because my sister disappeared. I know. I've thought about it a lot. The research suggests I'm solving my sister's disappearance with every case. But none bring me any healing. If anything, each one takes me farther away from it."

She leaned forward. "If you think this will bring you some healing, then I don't see anything wrong with it. But I want you to be prepared for what you find, Jon. You keep calling it a 'disappearance,' but you've told me before that you believe she was murdered. You may not like where this leads you. You need to be strong enough to handle what you find, or this will do more harm than good."

He nodded. "I've got one more case to finish up, then I'm heading up. I don't know what I'm going to find, but whatever it is, it has to be better than the things I picture in my head. I can't imagine that it's worse."

She leaned back and stared at him for a moment. "Sometimes, it's difficult for us to imagine the horror people really can do to each other—even for a homicide detective. Don't forget that up there, Jon."

"I won't." He rose. "I better go. Debbie's waiting for me. I'll call you when I get back."

As Stanton left, he looked at the Rothko painting again. It seemed different. The painting looked less ominous. Instead of falling or a tunnel, he saw mountains, water, and sky. He stood silently watching it for a second before leaving.

# EPILOGUE

The frigid air froze the snot in his nose. Richard's scarf kept slipping, and when he was tired of constantly pushing it up, he pulled out the full ski mask. His coat was puffy, and he was wearing thin gloves beneath a pair of thick Gore-Tex gloves. But the sun had set, and with the wind howling, the atmosphere was pretty much the epitome of arctic. He'd never enjoyed the cold. Not ever. But Alaska was the least likely place someone would look for him after his trip to Baja.

The little fishing vessel banked hard to the right, nearly toppling him. He glanced back at the flying bridge, and the man at the controls said, "Sorry."

He'd rented the vessel to take him across the bay. The big cities were too populated, Anchorage especially. Until he could get the plastic surgery and find somebody who could create a new identity for him, he thought it best to stick to the smaller towns. No one asked questions in little towns up here, and no one cared who he was. Alaska was too wild for anyone to care.

The problem was that working in the fishing and oil industries were the only jobs. And Richard had never been a manual laborer. He had a law degree, and he hoped that he could still be a lawyer after assuming his new identity, so he could do something he was accustomed to.

A cold gust of wind blew across the bay, and he had to squint. The boat was far enough from land that all he could see were the twinkling lights of the city where he had spent four months, trying to lie as low as possible. He'd rented a small room, taken his meals at the café next door, and otherwise stayed inside to read or watch television. When he got lonely, he visited the brothel close to the motel, or the girls came to him when he called.

He glanced up to the bridge to ask him how much farther, but no one was there. Suddenly, he realized that the rumbling of the engines underneath his feet had stopped. Richard looked into the cabin and didn't see anyone there. Then he heard footsteps.

Three men came up from below deck. Two came close to him, and Richard took a few steps back until he was pressed against the railing.

"What the hell are you doing? I rented this vessel."

They grabbed his arms.

"Hey! What're you doing! I chartered this damn boat. It's mine. Let go of me."

One of the men slammed his elbow into Richard's face, knocking him senseless. His jaw instantly burned, and pain shot through his head.

"You always did have a big mouth." The third man stood in front of him.

Richard looked up as the man lowered the mask covering his face. He lifted the glasses on his face, and Richard recognized him— Sharon's father, Eli.

"What're—how did you find me?"

"You think you're so fucking smart. That you just could kill my only daughter, and that a man of my means wouldn't do anything about it? You know what we called guys like you in Vietnam? We called you rabbits. 'Cause guys like you aren't good for anything but running."

"Eli, no… no, that's not true. I didn't hurt Sharon. I loved her. I would never hurt her. I was set up. You gotta believe me."

He sighed. "I told her not to marry you. I said you were gutless and that she needed someone strong. This is my fault, too, Richard. Maybe if I had pushed the issue, threatened her… something, she wouldn't have gone anywhere near you. So we're both to blame for this."

"No, Eli, listen to me. Eli, I did not kill her. I didn't do it. It was a set-up."

"Don't worry about Eliza. She's with me, and she'll never want for anything. And I sure as hell am gonna have a say in who she marries." He looked at one of the men. "Throw him in."

"No! Eli, no!"

Richard screamed, trying to break free. But he couldn't move. The men were much bigger and much stronger than he was. They lifted him as if he weighed nothing, and he felt his feet leave the deck.

"No. No! Eli, I didn't do it. Eli. Eli!"

He slammed into black, freezing water. Underwater, the world went silent, until his head thrust through the surface. Richard kicked and splashed with his thickly gloved hands as the water seeped into his coat and prickled his skin. It splashed up into his mouth and choked him. He saw the lights of the boat as the engine turned on, then it sped away from him.

"No!" he gurgled. "No! Eli, please. Please don't leave me. Eli!"

The water soaked his heavy clothes, making him feel as though he weighed three hundred pounds. He kicked furiously, but the effort needed to stay afloat was exhausting him. He reached down to take off his clunky snow boots, but his gloved fingers couldn't grasp the latch or the laces. He tried taking his gloves off. The instant the first one came off, his fingers felt as if they had been stuck in a freezer for an hour. A high wave hit him and pulled him under.

Water flooded his mouth and nose. He burst out of the surface again, coughing and gagging. He tried to suck in air, but as soon as he did so, another wave slammed into him and spun him. Underwater, he wasn't sure whether he was right side up or not. He tried to swim, but he couldn't get more than a few feet. His arms and legs had already become exhausted in the cold, and he had little willpower left. Within a few minutes, the cold had numbed him to the point of apathy.

And as he sank below the surface, Richard Miller looked up at the sky. His body dipped farther into the darkness, until he could no longer see the stars.

# AUTHOR'S REQUEST

If you enjoyed this book, please leave a review on Amazon.com. Good reviews not only encourage authors to write more, they improve our writing. Shakespeare rewrote sections of his plays based on audience reaction and modern authors should take a note from the Bard.

So please leave a review and know that I appreciate each and every one of you!

CPSIA information can be obtained
at www.ICGtesting.com
Printed in the USA
BVHW031153070720
583159BV00001B/21